The Bridge

Tales from a Revolution: Delaware

Also by Lars D. H. Hedbor,
available from Brief Candle Press:

The Prize: Tales From a Revolution - Vermont
The Light: Tales From a Revolution - New-Jersey
The Smoke: Tales From a Revolution - New-York
The Declaration: Tales From a Revolution - South-Carolina
The Break: Tales From a Revolution - Nova-Scotia
The Wind: Tales From a Revolution - West-Florida
The Darkness: Tales From a Revolution - Maine
The Path: Tales From a Revolution - Rhode-Island
The Freedman: Tales From a Revolution - North-Carolina
The Tree: Tales From a Revolution - New-Hampshire
The Mine: Tales From a Revolution - Connecticut
The Siege: Tales From a Revolution - Virginia
The Will: Tales From a Revolution - Pennsylvania
The Convention: Tales From a Revolution - Massachusetts
The Oath: Tales From a Revolution - Georgia
The Powder: Tales From a Revolution - Bermuda
The Word: Tales From a Revolution - Maryland

The Bridge

Lars D. H. Hedbor

Brief Candle
Press

Cover and book design: Brief Candle Press.
Cover image based on "Autumn Woods," Albert Bierstadt, 1866.
Map reproduction courtesy of Library of Congress, Geography and Map Division.
Fonts: Allegheney, Doves Type, and IM FELL English.

First Brief Candle Press edition published 2025.
www.briefcandlepress.com

ISBN: 978-1-942319-89-4

Dedication

Blessed are the peacemakers,
in every era

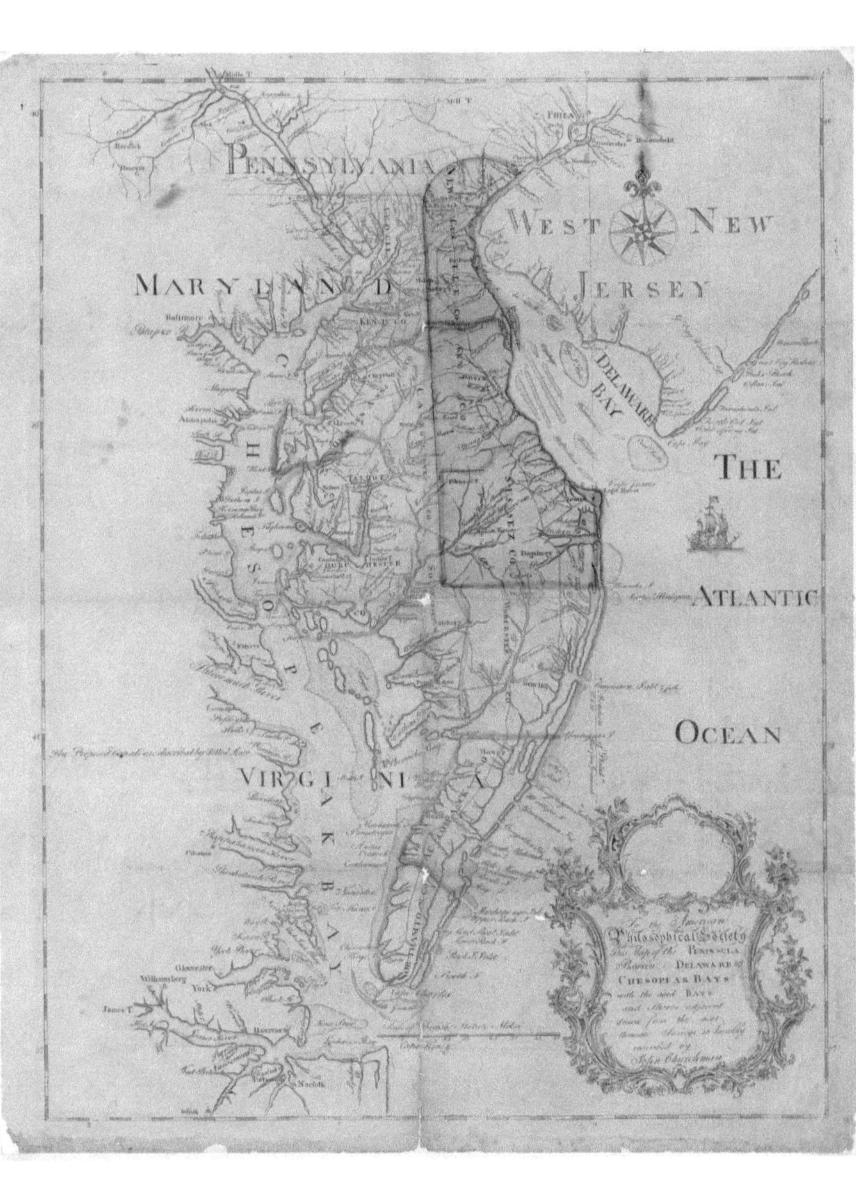

PENNSYLVANIA
MARYLAND
WEST NEW JERSEY
DELAWARE BAY
THE
ATLANTIC
OCEAN
VIRGINIA
CHESOPEAK BAY
Baltimore
Annapolis
Norfolk
Williamsburg
York
PHIL.
To the American Philosophical Society
This Map of the Peninsula
Between Delaware &
Chesopeak Bays
with the said Bays
and Shores adjacent
drawn from the most
accurate Surveys is humbly
inscribed by
John Churchman

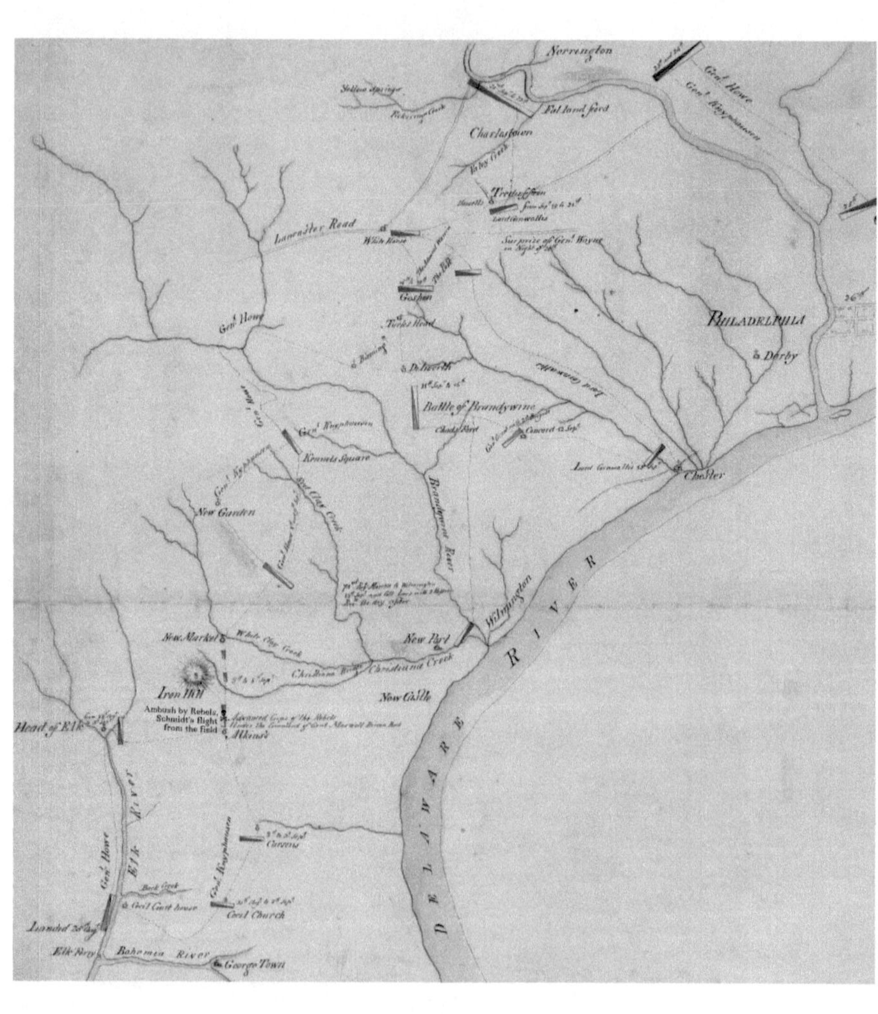

Norrengton
Yellow Springs
Pickering Creek
Val land ford
Charlestown
Valy Creek
Trederffrin
Howells
from 20 to 24
Landtonwallis
Lancaster Road
White Horse
Surprise of Genl Wayne
in Night of
The Fox
Goshen
Turks Head
Genl Howe
PHILADELPHIA
Derby
Battle of Brandywine
Genl Knyphausen
Chads Ford
Concord 12 Sep
Kennets Square
Lord Cornwallis
Red Clay Creek
Lord Cornwallis
Chester
New Garden
Brandywine River
Wilmington
New Market
New Port
White Clay Creek
Iron Hill
Christiana Creek
Christiana
New Castle
Ambush by Rebels,
Schmidt's flight
from the field
Advanced Corps of the Rebels
under the Command of Genl Maxwell Driven Back
Atkiss
Head of Elk
ELK RIVER
Genl Howe
Cuckens
Genl Knyphausen
Back Creek
Genl Greens House
Cool Church
Landed 28 Aug
Elk Ferry
Bohemia River
George Town
DELAWARE RIVER

Chapter I

The sound, like a swift, buzzing bee, passed by his ear and caught Caspar Schmidt's attention before the first crack of a musket's fire reached him. It wasn't until the man who had been glumly marching beside him fell groaning to the ground that he realized that the two noises had been associated, and that they were under attack.

There was no time to shoulder his own musket and return fire. Another volley sounded from the woods, and more men fell wounded around him. He heard an odd metallic bang as one man's high, decorative hat was struck by a musket ball, and Caspar dropped to the ground to avoid suffering the same fate. He rolled away from the muddy road and into the wet grass along the verge, the wild thought striking him that all of his attention to the cleanliness and upkeep of his uniform was now for naught.

He now heard his officers shouting orders and the deafening report of Hessian muskets finally answering the Americans, but the tall grass into which he'd rolled blocked his fellow soldiers from view. Indeed, he felt a curious sense of detachment from the action unfolding just a short distance from where he lay, the damp soaking through his clothing and reaching his skin.

All of his training should have driven him back to his feet, answering the call of his sergeant's crisp commands to load, present, and fire on the enemy. The fear of being seen as a deserter, and the brutal beating his entire company would deliver to him on his capture, should have brought him to his feet to emerge from the grass and stand by his fellows.

That buzzing sound recalled itself unbidden to his mind, though, and the reminder that sudden death had passed only a hand's breadth away from his head kept him still on the ground. Briefly, he wondered if he had been hit, and whether he lay there waiting for death to claim him, but he could feel no wound, and was troubled only by the strap of his musket digging into his neck as it pulled awkwardly under him.

He moved from his back to his knees to relieve that discomfort and found that he was even more concealed from the men still on the road than he'd originally thought. Somehow, he had not noticed that the land fell sharply away from the road where he'd rolled, so the grass at the top of the slope prevented him from being seen at all where he crouched.

Almost without volition, Caspar found himself moving further away from the road, toward a small clump of trees. His tall, distinctive hat was nowhere to be seen, and neither his musket nor his jacket or rucksack seemed important to keep, either. With his movement unencumbered by the outward indicators of his identity, he could crawl more quickly, and before he had really formed any intentional plan, he was among the trees, and able to see the action from a distance.

On the small hill to the left of the road where he and his company of dragoons had been marching, he could see men— American rebels—moving about openly, using the advantage of the high ground to aim and fire round after round at the now-retreating Hessian troops. Another body of American soldiers had formed up to block the way over the bridge that had formed the natural chokepoint they had relied upon to lay an ambush against the Hessians.

Caspar could just make out Captain Ewald himself, leading the retreat toward the bulk of the Hessian and British forces. He had little doubt that the move was only a temporary capitulation, as the main body of the British army would be along soon to drive the American ambush away.

Now, though, Caspar was content to watch his countrymen march briskly away, carrying with them the hope that he could pretend to be anything but a deserter.

He had never planned to be a soldier. Far less had he intended to become a plaything of distant princes, sent to fight in a war that had no possible effect on his little village in Hesse. The only thing he had wanted to be was a tailor.

His apprenticeship to Herr Drehnbacher had gone well, and he had learned everything that he should have needed to know to establish himself in the trade. However, once Drehnbacher had declared Caspar to be a journeyman tailor, there had been no shop with enough business to take on another set of hands. The question of starting his own shop had never even crossed his mind, so distant was that prospect.

Surviving on little more than the kindness of his mother's heart—though she had little enough of that to offer—when the prince's representative had come to the village to fill his quota, Caspar had quickly found himself conscripted into the service of the landgrave, available to any friendly nation that needed military forces.

When the sergeant had come into his platoon's barracks

with the news that Britain's King George had just concluded an arrangement with the landgrave to supplement his forces in the restive American colonies, most of the men around Caspar had taken the news with little comment, busying themselves with the details of preparing for their voyage.

Georg, a private who had been swept up in conscription a year before Caspar, reflected the prevailing phlegmatic opinion of the matter when Caspar asked him about it.

With a shrug that barely moved the shoulders of his over-sized jacket, Georg said, "It is only what we are here for, Herr Schmidt. The landgrave must fill his coffers somehow, and we must fill our bellies. He gets paid by the British king, and so we get paid by him. This is the way that the world works."

He turned back to neatly folding and packing his freshly issued clothing, and Caspar had grimaced and applied himself to the same task. It was true that he had more money now than he ever had as an apprentice, and that the outfit he had been issued consisted of the sturdiest new-made items he had ever owned.

Whatever fortunate tailor had earned the contract to outfit the regiment had taken pride in doing so, using quality wool fabric, sewn by men who knew their trade well. Even as only a journeyman, Caspar could see the care that had been taken in the stitching and trimming, and expected to wear these clothes for many years to come.

Remembering the moment when he'd first handled the finely made regimental coat, Caspar couldn't help but snort at himself for how easily he had abandoned it to molder in some American field. As he stood and pushed himself away from the trees where he had concealed himself, he hoped that someone might find the things he'd left behind, and make better use of them than he had.

Now, though, he needed to get as far from this field of battle as he could, while the dragoons were occupied with summoning help from the main army. Having committed himself this far to desertion, he had little alternative but to finish the job. That meant putting as much distance as he could between himself and the site that would doubtless soon witness a renewed clash.

Falling into the steady trot he'd been trained to use when the need arose to move quickly, he made good time over the countryside, leaving the accursed bridge and the strategic hill overlooking it far behind.

By the time his legs were aching from being on the move for so long, and he'd twisted one ankle in an unseen burrow of some sort, Caspar was grateful beyond all measure to see a small farm below as he crested a small rise. The farmer and his hands were nowhere in evidence, and Caspar found the barn unlocked and unguarded.

Taking refuge in the rafters to avoid being instantly spotted, he huddled down into his arms and settled against a stout, roughly hewn post to get the first proper sleep he had enjoyed in weeks.

He awoke to the drumming of rain against the roof overhead, and his opinion of the farmer rose considerably as he realized he was both warm and dry, despite his cramped posture. The roof was tight, and without leaks—good not only for the livestock whose presence he could smell from his perch, but also for Caspar's purposes.

He re-arranged himself to get more comfortable, and went back to sleep, serene in the knowledge that he was safe from both the elements and from anyone who might have been dispatched to pursue suspected deserters, as unlikely as that seemed.

When Caspar woke up again, the rain had stopped, but the air had taken on an evening chill. He was just pondering coming down from the rafters when the door to the barn swung open, and the farmer appeared, leading in two cattle.

Caspar held still, but observed the man with curiosity. This was the first American he had seen up close, and he wanted to glean anything he could from observing his unwitting host.

The farmer was speaking to the animals in low, comforting tones, but he was, naturally enough, using English. Caspar's knowledge of the language was only slight—only what might be necessary to answer the most basic of questions posed by an English-speaking customer at a tailor's shop—but he strained his ears anyway, hoping that he might pick up something of use.

At first, the farmer seemed to be preoccupied with coaxing the cows into their respective pens. His tone in speaking to them shifted from quiet and persuasive to holding an edge of irritation as the second animal balked at its door. Perhaps the problem was that Caspar was nearly directly overhead of that spot, or, he supposed, it might be that the farmer's topic of conversation had shifted.

Caspar could pick out the names of a few military commanders on both sides in the farmer's stream of words, and he wondered whether the man was commenting on the events of the day. The farmer's tone grew sharper, and his hand slashed through the air in his agitation.

Picking up on the man's changing tone of voice, the first cow now also set her feet firmly, refusing to move forward into her pen. Caspar could see the man's chest swell, and he braced himself for the outburst he just knew would follow.

Instead, the farmer directed his eyes upward and blew out a long, slow breath. Although the man was facing away from where he was huddled, Caspar froze, willing himself to absolute stillness, terrified that the farmer's upward glance would reveal his dark form amongst the rafters.

When the farmer looked down, seemingly seeing nothing untoward in his effort to regain control over himself, Caspar permitted himself to breathe again, but only just barely.

Once he heard the man speaking in a calm, collected voice to his cows, Caspar relaxed just a hair. The animals, too, seemed to relax at the farmer's less stringent tone, and cooperated in his attempts to lead them into their stalls.

Only once the cows were contentedly chewing their cuds in the darkness, and it had been a long while since the farmer had departed, did Caspar feel his way back to the narrow ladder he'd climbed up. The barn door's long, mournful creak had taken another year from Caspar's life when he closed it behind himself, but he slipped away into the drizzly night undetected, determined to find a safer refuge from which he could begin his new life in America.

Chapter 2

The early winter afternoon light slanting into the millinery shop provided little warmth, but made it hard for Caspar to make out who had swung open the door and stepped in. However, the man's exuberant movements and broad, sturdy form gave him away even before he opened his mouth.

"Mister Jacobson, it is good to see you this day," Caspar called out, a smile breaking out over his face. Though six years had given him a comfortable command of the English language, he remained self-conscious about his heavy accent with most people. Karl Jacobson was not one of them.

"It is wonderful to see you today, as well, my friend. This is a day that I hope you will remember to the end of your own time. News has just arrived from Paris that the government has finally concluded the peace with Britain. The war is, at last, officially over."

Somewhere between Caspar's shoulders, a knot of tension abruptly dissolved. Until that very moment, he had not been aware that he had carried it ever since that day when the tall grass had blocked off his view of the rest of the company of Hessian dragoons, but its sudden removal almost made him gasp in relief.

"Over, you say? There will no longer be any threat that the English king might change his mind, or that his Parliament might be taken over by men who want to try again to take back their colonies?"

"No, indeed. Here, I brought a copy of the Gazetteer, which is come up from Philadelphia. It reproduces the complete text of the final treaty." He drew a hastily folded broadsheet out of his jacket pocket and laid it on the counter, smoothing it out for Caspar's examination.

"There," he said, stabbing his fingertip at a dense column of text. "Those are the terms, signed, sealed, and delivered up to Congress."

Caspar peered closely at the closely spaced lines of text. His lips moved as he sounded out some of the more difficult words, but Jacobson waited patiently, respecting his need to work through the challenging text on his own.

He skimmed over the preamble, moved on through the description of where the frontier lay between the territory of the United States and England's remaining North American holdings, and read with mild interest the concessions to American fishing rights in the great banks along Nova Scotia and Newfoundland. That was of only passing personal interest, though, as he preferred venison or beef over the dried cod that those fisheries delivered to the markets.

Reaching the articles that dealt with debts and restoration of properties, he slowed down to see if there were any terms that might formally clarify the status of men who, like himself, had once served the King of England, but had stopped doing so under irregular circumstances. When he had found nothing by the end of the text, he shrugged and looked up at Jacobson, offering the broadsheet back to him.

"It appears the king was obliged to concede nearly

everything we could have wished. You are correct, my friend. This is a day to remember. The war is over, and we have won our place among the nations of the world."

"Just so, Mister Schmidt." The other man paused as he finished folding the newspaper and slipping it back into his pocket. "Are the children here? I should like to share our joy with them, and with my daughter."

"Of course." He turned to the stairs behind the counter and called up, "Karin! Tell the children that their *morfar* is here, and would like to see them."

His wife's answering voice sounded sweetly from above, "Please tell him we will need a few moments to ready ourselves, and then we will be down." Caspar's face assumed a gentle smile.

He turned back to Jacobson, still smiling. "I think they might even be freshly washed, since Bjorn somehow found some mud to put into his and his sister's hair this morning." He shook his head. "Karin was quite cross with them both."

Jacobson grinned in reply. "It is the way of all children, particularly when family comes to call. I remember well one time when my old *farfar* was down from Wilmington and I came in from the field with my little brother, having just persuaded him to swallow a live cricket. I had lied to him and told him it would eat up the turnips our mother was making for supper, but only if he could still feel it wiggling inside his belly. He hated turnips, you see."

The older man guffawed at the memory and said, "He could feel it wiggling inside, but it turned out that he could not keep it there long enough to eat his turnips. Our *farfar* had just picked him up when the cricket and everything else in Knut's belly came back up all at once, all over *Farfar's* face."

Caspar closed his eyes and covered his mouth, trying to contain the bark of mirth that threatened to escape. "Oh, *mein Gott*," he chortled behind his hand. "I will ask you to never tell that story where Bjorn can hear it. He has ideas enough of his own."

Jacobson placed a finger over his mouth and somehow brought his laughter under control. "I'll never share it where he can hear it. You have my word. *Farfar* had come over from the old country as a little boy, and had seen his share of seasickness and illness, but he told me many years later that this incident was the worst thing he had ever experienced in his entire life."

He looked thoughtful and added, "I suppose it is little wonder that he left nothing to me, but gave Knut a generous bequest. Nobody can keep a grudge like an old Swede."

Just then, Karin descended the narrow, steep stairs, stepping carefully and carrying their daughter Lena. Behind them, Bjorn climbed down, facing the stairs and holding on as he stepped down each one in turn. Karin smiled widely as her father stepped forward and caught Lena, who had launched herself toward her grandfather's arms as soon as she saw him.

Once he had the toddler settled on his hip, he accepted a kiss on the cheek from Karin. "How is my favorite daughter today, and my favorite granddaughter?"

"Your only daughter and only granddaughter are doing very well, thank you, Pappa," she said, adding, "All the better now that I washed the children."

Bjorn finished descending the stairs and charged over to grab his grandfather around the legs. "I was making our hair dark like Betje's." He made a sour face as he stepped back and pointed to his head. "She said that we look like we have flax growing on our heads."

Patting the boy's head and tousling his white-blond hair, Jacobson said, "You both have the same beautiful hair that your mamma had when she was your age. This Betje doesn't sound like she is very nice."

Karin said, "Oh, she's fine, just her parents are Dutch, and you know how they still feel about *Nya Sverige*. More than one hundred years it has been since they conquered our little colony, and they won't let us forget it."

Jacobson raised an eyebrow and turned back to Caspar. "I may need to reconsider what I said earlier. No Swede can hold a grudge like the Dutch."

Caspar laughed and shook his head, raising his hands as though in surrender. "I won't even try to make a case that an old German can do more, but I suspect that my mother still hasn't forgiven me for never writing her any letter, even though she could not read it."

Feeling the mood shift to something too serious, he continued, "But you come bringing joyous news, which you should share with my family."

Jacobson said, "I do, yes." He tapped his pocket significantly. "I have word from Philadelphia today that the war is finally completely concluded, and that the peace is signed. We have now to make our own way as a nation in the world."

Karin nodded serenely. "It had to come to pass sooner or later. General Washington brought their armies to heel, and the King had no choice but to sue for peace. I am surprised only that it took men so long to recognize the facts as they stood."

Jacobson smiled. "If only the diplomats were as sensible as my daughter."

Chapter 3

Caspar heard the shop door open and looked up from the waistcoat whose back he was just about finished stitching together. The man who had entered had a thin face, almost to the point of gauntness, and his eyes darted around in the manner of one who has had to depend upon his alertness for survival.

Putting the waistcoat aside, Caspar rose from the comfortable tailor's seat position in which he habitually worked, and stepped down from the table. He called out to the stranger, "Welcome to my shop, sir. What can I do for you?"

The man's restless eyes settled on Caspar, and he answered with an accent so thick that it made Caspar realize just how far his English had come. "I need a new breeches, please. I am too thin for these become."

Caspar answered in German, "Please, do not fear to speak our own language. We will understand each other more easily, yes?"

The stranger looked startled, but nodded after a moment. "Yes, please. With the peace, our company was released from our imprisonment. Some of us decided it would be better to stay here than to return to our own country."

Caspar nodded encouragingly. "A wise choice you have made. This is a land filled with opportunity. Now, about those breeches?"

"Yes, of course. You may have heard that the camps for captured soldiers struggled to secure foodstuffs and supplies for our maintenance. I have heard it said that it was worse for us from Hesse than for the English, but in any event, I can lace these no tighter, and yet they fall off my body."

He turned to show Caspar that the lacing below the small of his back that allowed breeches to be made to one size and fitted to individual wearers was, in fact, pulled all the way in. With his thumb, he pulled the side of the waist out, demonstrating that it left enough slack that an incautious move could actually let them fall to his knees.

Caspar looked over the breeches with a critical, practiced eye. If the material weren't so worn, dirty, and haphazardly patched, he might suggest simply adjusting the seams at the sides to take them in, but that would only delay the inevitable, without giving this man the new article of clothing he needed for a new start.

Nodding, he said, "Step up onto this stool, so that I can measure you."

The soldier did as he was instructed, and Caspar cut a long, thin strip of paper with which to record the necessary fit. Working efficiently, he moved the strip around the man's waist, folded it where his fingers held the measurement, and used a pair of shears to nip a diamond out of it along the fold.

He moved briskly, likewise marking the lengths he would need to cut the fabric to the right size for a pair of breeches that would fit this man's body perfectly. Finished, he offered his hand to help the stranger down, and motioned with his head to the counter. "Come, join me here and we can discuss what cloth you want me to use, and how much it will cost."

Stopping at the counter, he looked shrewdly at the man and asked, "You do have money?"

The man smiled grimly. "I have only the continental dollars we were given when we were released. They told us they must be accepted under the law, but I have heard many men of the prison garrison complaining about how little they could purchase."

Caspar pursed his mouth. "There is much truth to those complaints, but I will tell you prices in continental currency, so that we may know what you can afford, yes?"

"Yes," the stranger said, his manner suddenly hesitant. "And if it is too much, perhaps I can find some other means by which I can pay for them."

Caspar said nothing, but he knew that Karin would have no patience for him offering charity to a customer, particularly if she sensed the offer was made out of sympathy for a former countryman.

He had turned to pull fabric options from his shelves when he heard the stranger gasp. "You are Caspar Schmidt?"

He turned back to the soldier, that familiar knot between his shoulders tensing up again in an instant. Hesitantly, he said, "Yes, that is my name."

The man nodded, a scowl on his face. "I did not recognize you. It has been so long since I thought you were killed at the bridge, but when you turned, it came to me who you are."

He pulled himself up to his full height, his eyes flashing. "I am Sigmund Graff, and I was your sergeant that day. While you have been playing with cloth and paper and growing fat, I have been fighting as my officers have commanded, and then starving in a prison camp until just a fortnight ago."

Now it was Caspar's time to gasp, as he recognized the sergeant's hard eyes now that they were trained on him in a familiar flinty, angry scowl. The years had not been kind to Graff, and the conditions in the prison camp had taken a toll on more than just his once-robust frame. Now that the man had assumed a more military bearing, Caspar realized it hadn't been just his eyes that had been uncertain and ready to react to danger.

Where he now stood with a ramrod-straight spine, his arms crossed tightly over his chest, he had previously been in a wary crouch, his hands free to defend himself from any attack. Caspar could remember having to consciously overcome his own tendency to walk like that in the months after his irregular departure from military service. It had seemed to him that every shadow could conceal the threat of being dragged back to face the consequences of his departure.

And now, he felt that familiar fear come crashing back over him as he faced his former military superior. He slumped over the counter, his hands over his mouth, as he pondered his reply.

Finally, he lifted his head and answered the other man, "Sergeant, those were the actions of a terrified and confused youth, exposed for the first time in his existence to the possibility of immediate death. Yes, I have made a life for myself here, and have left that scared boy behind in the ditch where he fell. We stand before each other now as fellow citizens of a new nation, not as superior and subject. The war is in the past; let us leave it there."

Graff's nostrils flared, but he said nothing for a long moment, his gaze seemingly taking Caspar's measure, and finding him lacking. Caspar had sweated through many an inspection and drill under that same gaze, and had never felt as though he measured up to its expectations.

That feeling had not changed in the six years since he'd last experienced it, and when Graff finally spoke, his words were nearly as harsh a blow as they had been then.

"The war is past, yes. However, one of us stood by his fellow soldiers in facing that enemy, even at the risk to our own lives, health, and safety. One of us remembered the promises we had made, and fought for the cause we had been commanded to defend."

His eyes swept over the tidy shop, its bright fabrics folded neatly on shelves, work in process sitting in orderly progression on the table, and clean windows admitting sunlight to warm the cat curled on the sill.

He returned his gaze to consider Caspar and continued, "The other of us abandoned his friends to die at the enemy's hands, and then made himself comfortable among that enemy. The other of us betrayed his country and his own honor, for the cheap comfort of a little shop in a quiet town, among people whose dishonorable and brutal conduct in the war you overlooked for a pat on the head and a piece of cheese, like any common rat."

Caspar felt his ears burning with the flush that had overcome him, and he hated that his reaction to the other man's verbal attack had to have been so obviously visible. The worst of it was that there was little in Graff's accusations that he had not leveled at himself in those first awful months after his desertion.

His sleep was often interrupted by reliving the pained groan of the man who had fallen beside him when the American forces had sprung their ambush on the Hessian dragoons. Other times, the buzz of the bullet had come closer, ever closer, until he awoke gasping and drenched in sweat.

The dreamlike state that had overtaken him when he had dropped over the side of the road had never really made sense to him, but his deliberate actions in the days afterward were purposeful and considered, all pursuing the goal of leaving behind the battle that he knew had nearly claimed his life, and taking him as far as possible away from any possibility of experiencing it again.

His meeting with Karin and their courtship had sometimes been marred by pangs of guilt that he suffered when he would hear news of some Hessian company or another—sometimes even mentioning Captain Ewald's command by name—suffered losses or defeats. The joy that he found in their marriage was tempered by the knowledge that all around the continent surrounding them, men pined for their wives and sweethearts, while he had his beside him.

The kind support of his new friends and neighbors when he had been striving to start his shops had astounded him, and he had worked hard to be worthy of their trust and generosity, aware that he had found no such consideration in his hometown. It seemed of little importance that the men who had fired on his company had come from among the ranks of those among whom he now lived. They had their cause, and it was one that he had come to understand and support himself, persuaded that it was just and right.

He raised his eyes from where they had been avoiding Graff's and answered him. "I can understand how you can see things that way, Sergeant Graff. However, the past cannot be changed. It remains only as a source to inform us and, hopefully, offer wisdom. I do not regret that I have the place in this life that I have built here. Whatever errors I have made, I have earned the happiness and comfort I have found here."

His eyes flashing with open disdain, Graff turned on his heel toward the door. He paused before leaving, saying coldly, "I find, Herr Schmidt, that I do not need new breeches after all. These will serve me better than any that come from the hands of a traitor."

Chapter 4

Caspar tried to shake off the confrontation with his old sergeant, but even after he bolted the door to the shop and climbed the stairs into the house, he could still feel the old ball of tension between his shoulders. His anxiety must have been written clearly on his face, because Karin exclaimed as soon as he entered the kitchen.

"What is troubling you, my dear? You look as though something terrible has happened."

Caspar shook his head quickly in dismissal. "It is likely nothing, but my old sergeant just appeared at our door, and made the most unpleasant accusations against me."

"Your old sergeant? You mean, from when you were a soldier?"

"Exactly so," Caspar answered. "He thought I had died in the ambush at Cooch's Bridge, and when he perceived who I was, he called me a traitor and said that I had abandoned my fellow soldiers to their fates when I ran."

Karin began to speak, her manner making it clear that she wanted to offer him reassurance, but he raised his hand to forestall her predictable support, welcome though it was.

"The truth of the matter is that I cannot tell myself with any certainty that he is wrong. I took care of my own safety, without regard for the fates of the other members of the company. In doing so, I betrayed the oath I gave—however unwillingly—to obey the orders I was given and to fight in the name of my landgrave."

He bit his lip pensively. "You should have seen him, Karin. He had been held as a captive, and had come to the nearest millinery for breeches that would fit his reduced frame. He commented, too, on my having grown fat while he went hungry."

Finally, he relented and went to his wife's arms, taking comfort in her embrace. After a long moment, she pulled back slightly and took him by both elbows.

"I will not hear you speak of regret for the choices that brought you to my life, and that gave me my good, conscientious husband, and our children their father." Caspar was surprised to see her eyes well up now, as she was usually one to keep her emotions firmly in check.

She released one of his elbows just long enough to wipe away an angry tear. "I was not there when you ran, but I have never seen you lack for courage in the face of difficulty. War is not the only way in which a man can prove his worth, and you serve your countrymen better as an honest craftsman than as a plaything of princes far away."

Now Karin released his arms and visibly brought herself back under control. "I will hear no more of your guilt for the good fortune you have earned. Dinner is nearly ready for the table, and you still need to wash."

Dinner was subdued for both parents, though Bjorn was in high spirits, and more than once, Karin had to remind him to attend to his porridge and not his fanciful tales.

Caspar's attention was drawn away from the conflict that roiled in his mind between his old commander's words and his wife's, when Bjorn announced, "Betje said that our English is not so fine as hers, because Papa is from another country, and her family has been here for a hundred years."

Although he could only remember meeting this Betje once in passing, he was already developing a hearty dislike for the child, and to harbor suspicions that her parents must be saying many terrible things in her presence, for her to repeat to his children.

Karin answered briskly, "She is probably just jealous that my family has been here in America for longer than hers. But more importantly, she has not yet learned that boasting only tells people what you feel inadequate about in yourself."

Seeing the confusion on the boy's face, she said, "That just means that she has probably been scolded for her English, so she tells you that yours is not as good as hers to make herself feel better."

Bjorn considered this for a moment, a frown on his face. "That doesn't make any sense, Mama."

"No, it doesn't," Caspar said. "But your mama is right—many times, people don't make much sense when they're being mean." It struck him as he said it that he could easily apply these words of supposed wisdom to himself, but he dismissed the thought. The cases were not parallel, after all.

Bjorn nodded solemnly. "I will tell Betje tomorrow that she has worse English that we do, and that she won't make hers better by telling us ours is not good."

Caspar choked back a laugh, and Karin said sharply, "You will do no such thing, Bjorn. Being mean to someone who is mean to you only makes you both mean, and doesn't solve anything."

Caspar intoned, "You listen to your mother, and listen to

how she talks, too. You will speak better than Betje if you speak like your mother, and that is a better way to prove your friend wrong than by just telling her she is wrong, you see?"

Bjorn looked thoughtful again and finally nodded his agreement. "But if she is mean to Lena again, I will tell her to stop it."

"And you should," Caspar said. "She is bigger than Lena, and does not need to tease your sister. It is good to watch over those who need protection. But you are bigger than Betje, so you should also not tease her."

Bjorn protested, "I do not tease her, Papa!"

Karin stepped into the conversation before it could get even more out of hand. "Good. See that you don't. Nothing makes a person's meanness more evident than when she is the only one being mean."

Lena picked this moment to speak up. "Bjorn nice! He give me snowballs."

Bjorn looked suddenly worried, and Caspar just knew that there was more to this story. Karin said innocently, "That does sound nice, sweet heart. What did you do with the snowballs?"

Lena giggled. "Throw them at Bet-lay" The toddler had not yet mastered the combination of sounds needed to pronounce Betje's name correctly, but that was not what made Caspar frown as he turned back to Bjorn.

For his part, the boy had sunk down on the bench and appeared to be in danger of sliding entirely off of it, to disappear completely under the table. "Sit up straight," Caspar snapped. "And what is this about throwing snowballs at Betje?"

Sullenly, the boy complied, and answered, "She said that

we couldn't hit her, because our eyes were too pale and there was no way we could see properly."

Caspar sighed. He was going to have to have words with Betje's parents, he could see, and try to convince them to stop sharing their nonsensical ideas with their daughter.

For the moment, though, he decided to try to get to the truth of today's incident. "Did she tell you to hit her with snowballs?"

"Not exactly," Bjorn said, evasively.

"What did she say, exactly?"

"She said, 'I bet you can't even hit me from the other side of the street.' Lena couldn't, but I did, right in the back of her head."

Again, Caspar had to stifle laughter, and he said, mildly, "That isn't quite the same as telling you to try."

Karin added, "Even if she did say that you should try to hit her, *I* say that you should never try to hit someone with anything."

The boy looked stubborn for a moment, and Caspar chimed in to support his wife. "Anyone can hit a little girl with a snowball. It takes a good person, though, to decide not to, no matter how much it feels like she deserves it."

Karin gave her husband a sour look. "Nobody ever deserves to be hit with something, and if someone were to throw a snowball at you, I would expect you to try to not let them hit you instead of returning their bad behavior. There is nothing at all wrong about running away from someone who is trying to hurt you."

Suddenly, Caspar didn't think that her comments were entirely about a snowball fight any more. For his part, Bjorn's face had only grown more stubborn-looking.

Finally, the boy could contain himself no more. "So you want me to run away from a girl, even if she is throwing things at

Lena and I could stop her?"

Caspar let his face fall into his hands for a moment before answering carefully. "If you can keep your little sister safer by running away with her from someone who is trying to hurt either of you, there is nothing wrong with doing that. Only if you cannot run away, should you consider whether you need to stop Betje by throwing something at her yourself."

The boy scoffed. "Betje's daddy said that you know all about running away."

Caspar felt his blood run cold, and he heard Karin gasp beside him. She snapped, "Bjorn, leave this table, and do not think to come back to eat at it again until you have made an apology to your father."

Bjorn burst into tears, but did as he was instructed. Caspar turned to his wife and said, "You probably just saved that boy a thrashing, when the one who deserves it is that Willem van Dusen."

She said quietly, "I know. It would do Bjorn no good for you to give him the paddling I know you want to, and it will do Betje's father no good for you to confront him, either."

Her mouth pressed into a grim line. "The children will not be playing with that little girl anymore, though, I can tell you that."

Still trying to master his anger, Caspar asked, "Do people really think that of me? Am I widely believed to be shy of danger, hiding behind my scissors and needle to avoid the battlefield?"

He didn't give voice to the larger fear he felt — were they right to feel that way about him? After all, the only time he had faced an enemy shooting at him, he had, in fact, run away. Was he so angry because the accusation held a painful kernel of truth?

Karin interrupted this bitter train of thought, saying, "The van Dusens hold more contempt for my family as Swedes than they do for your past. Her father likely only said such an ugly thing about you because he needs to believe that the Dutch are better, and so he will invent reasons to justify looking down on us."

She reached over and took his hand. "The man I married is worth ten of him, Caspar. Whether you are proud of your decisions in the past or not, you are a hard worker, an honest tradesman, and a good husband and father. The past is done and we cannot change it. What matters is how you have made something of yourself, despite many difficulties that you had to overcome."

Caspar wished that he could convince himself so readily of the truth of his wife's opinion of him, and wondered whether there was some coincidence that had brought both the sergeant's bitter words and their neighbor's foul comments to his ears on the same day.

Chapter 5

The next morning dawned under a sullen gray sky, and it seemed to perfectly reflect Caspar's mood as he opened up the shop for the day. The cat—kept primarily for his prowess at keeping the mice in check that might otherwise chew up fabric—looked up resentfully at his noisy arrival, obviously wishing for more time to snooze in peace.

Caspar favored the animal with a wry grimace and said, "Ah, Dolf, you would rather sleep than face this day? Well, we are not given that choice, are we? You must hunt your mice, and I must sew my seams."

The cat rose and lazily stretched, looking up at Caspar and giving him a curt "meow" before jumping down and rubbing against his master's leg on his way to leap up onto the stool in the corner, where he curled up and immediately went back to sleep.

Caspar shook his head and lit a few lanterns to supplement the dim light of the winter morning. Then he stepped up onto the table, reaching for the unfinished waistcoat, and resumed the fussy work of the finish stitching along the visible front seam of the lapel.

Though the work was painstaking, it required little of his active attention, so practiced were his movements with needle and thimble. His mind wandered back to the upsetting conversations of the prior day. Bjorn was outwardly contrite that morning—though Caspar suspected he was more hungry than truly sorry for the cruel comment he had passed along—and Karin had relented and let him join them for morning porridge.

He hoped his wife was right, and that van Dusen's attitude was not more widespread in the community. He had come to the realization during the night that it seemed unlikely, given how his neighbors and friends had come together to help him open the shop. Men did not extend a hand of friendship and encouragement in public and then turn around and sow doubt in private.

Thinking back, he recalled that van Dusen had not been among those who had helped, and he remembered Karin explaining something about a long-running dispute between his family and hers. Caspar suspected from her tone that there was more to the story, but he had not pressed her for details.

He could largely dismiss van Dusen from his mind, though convincing his children to shun Betje might be more difficult. There were, after all, only so many children of a similar age in the neighborhood.

His sergeant's appearance the prior day was a more distressing concern. Even if he could shake off the self-doubt that the man had triggered, his presence in the community would doubtless serve to remind those who might have forgotten of Caspar's shameful past.

No matter how Caspar might have wanted to follow Karin's admonition to leave the past in the past and worry about the future instead, he could not help but replay in his mind that awful moment when a bullet's passage by his ear had driven him to flee, and the months that had followed immediately after it.

His arrival in the town had aroused little comment at the time. His hunger had driven him to overcome his fear, and he had entered the public house. After a fumbling attempt to ask for a meal, someone motioned him to silence and led him to a table.

Although the tavern keeper offered him nothing but some weak ale, another man returned with an elderly man who had some German. After a brief, halting conversation, the old man called out to the tavern keeper, and the man brought him a bowl of thin broth.

It was the most delicious thing that Caspar could remember ever tasting, and even now, remembering it made his mouth water. It tasted of fowl—perhaps squab—and warmed Caspar from his belly out to his numbed toes.

The broth had been followed with another weak ale, and more broken conversation with the old man. He had asked Caspar bluntly, "You are to run from your troop?"

Caspar hesitated, and then nodded, his cheeks flushing in embarrassment. "I did not mean to desert—to run—but by the time I came to my senses, I was already so far away that my return would have made more trouble than simply continuing to run."

The old man nodded, waving a hand in an understanding dismissal, though Caspar was fairly confident that he had understood only the rudiments of his comment.

"We are asking no questions, only ask you if you to work will."

Caspar had hesitated, unsure that he'd fully grasped the other man's broken German. Finally, he nodded emphatically. "I will work." He pantomimed sewing and added, "I am a tailor."

The old man's smile convinced Caspar that he'd made himself understood clearly, so he summoned the courage to ask, "Is there a tailor in town who needs help?"

The old man considered his question, seeming not to have understood, so Caspar tried again. "Have you a tailor in the town?"

"I do not know this word, 'tailor,'" the other man confessed.

Again, Caspar mimed passing a needle through cloth, this time, directing its imaginary through the seam along his sleeve.

This time, the old man's smile was more brilliant. "Ah, yes, I know now this word. There is no tailor in the town, no. We must to buy clothes in Wilmington, or our wives to make ourselves."

"Maybe I can solve that problem," Caspar had said, and indeed, before the year was out, the old man had been one of the first to loan him money to get his start. At first, he had plied his trade in the public house, giving the tavern keeper a share of his earnings in exchange for the use of a table to discuss business with customers, and a room in which he both worked and slept.

Karin had been one of his first customers, brought by her father to order a new set of stays. He had enough English by that time to stammer and sweat his way through the delicate matter of getting her measurements, and her sweet smile and faint blush when she understood that she made him nervous had sent his heart soaring.

By the time he had delivered the finished article to her, he determined to stammer and sweat his way through asking her father for permission to court her. Mister Jacobson had grinned widely and answered, "If you do not, you will answer to me for her disappointment."

The courtship had developed in a tumbling, joyful sequence of meals taken with the Jacobson family, quieter walks alone with Karin through the streets of the town, and Sundays in church on the family pew. When the time came to announce the banns of marriage, Mister Jacobson had taken Caspar aside after the church service and asked him, "Would you walk with me, my young friend? I have something I should like to show you."

Caspar had been puzzled but had simply said, "Yes, certainly."

His prospective father-in-law had led him to an empty shop on a quieter side street, and had asked, "If you were operating from this location, rather than the tavern, would your customers still find you, do you think?"

Caspar's heart was in his throat as he answered, "I cannot think of why they would not, but I do not have enough business yet to even dream of a place like this."

Jacobson had guffawed and said, "I have paid the first year of rent on it as a dowry for you. By one year, I think you will have the business."

His father-in-law had been right, though the space upstairs from the shop had proven to be less roomy than it had first looked, with the addition of Bjorn and then Lena to the family. Although some of his early clientele appeared to have been sent his way by Jacobson, the training Caspar had received as an apprentice, together with the care that he put into his work became more widely known in the community.

Now, with the war over and what seemed like unlimited opportunity ahead of him, Sergeant Graff's sudden appearance at his door threatened to undo the sense of safety and belonging Caspar had developed.

He sighed and held up the finished waistcoat seam to the light from the tapers, inspecting it. Satisfied, he turned to the next task, hardly noticing the passage of the day outside. Though his customers did find him here without difficulty, casual passersby were relatively rare, and he found he liked the quiet for being able to focus on his work uninterrupted.

Usually uninterrupted, at least. The door swung open, and a man stepped in, a gust of wind coming in with him and blowing out one of the tapers. Trying to keep the irritation out of his expression, Caspar looked up to see who was calling, and immediately found himself more than irritated.

Willem van Dusen stood in the doorway, his hands on his hips, and glaring at Caspar. Another cold gust blew past him through the open door and extinguished the other candle. Caspar said crisply, "Come in and leave the winter outside, if you please, Mister van Dusen."

The man stood for another insolent moment, and then stepped fully inside and slammed the door behind himself.

"What is the meaning, Mister Schmidt, of letting your brat throw ice at my Betje?"

"I had understood that she provoked him by telling him that his eyes would not work well enough for him to aim well at her." Caspar could see no point in feigning civility with this man, who had clearly schooled his child in the article of insults.

Van Dusen's face grew stormier yet, and his voice rose nearly to a shout. "So you have heard about this assault, and have done nothing to reign in your boy's monstrous behavior?"

"My son's discipline is really none of your affair, Mister van Dusen, but I will assure you he will not be throwing any more snowballs at your daughter. Her conduct has made it clear that she is not a fit companion for my children."

"Her conduct!" Van Dusen's voice shook with rage. "I

came here to tell you to keep your dirty offspring away from Betje anyway, but to have you blame her for their misdeeds is altogether too much, sir!"

Caspar maintained a calm outward demeanor, and shrugged, saying, "Your daughter repeats a lot of things that she has apparently absorbed with her mother's milk. Foul prejudices about my children's mother, for example, and her heritage from good men and women."

He hesitated for a moment, and then decided that there was nothing to lose by adding, "It seems, also, that she has heard you call me a coward often enough that she saw fit to repeat that to my son."

Van Dusen initially seemed surprised to suddenly find himself the subject of criticism, but he lifted his chin and said, "Deny if it you will, sir. You were sent here to defend King George's rightful dominion over these colonies, and at the first hint of real danger, you abandoned your duty to king and country. Tell me, sir what would you call someone who did such a thing?"

In that moment, Caspar had two realizations, either of which alone would have been enough to leave him staggered, but which together, were somehow comforting. First, van Dusen was a Loyalist, clinging to fealty to a King who had relinquished his claim over this country. And second, his own flight from the field of battle had been not an act of cowardice, but the first step on the path to becoming an American.

His was the side of the angels, and van Dusen's anger, the ugly words repeated by his daughter, were the acts of a man lashing out on realizing that what he believed in deeply was a hollow shell, a lost cause.

Not that he was willing to tolerate the man's behavior, and he decided that there was only one proper answer to the accusation that he was shy. He had stepped toward van Dusen, preparing himself to slap him and issue a challenge of honor, when Karin's voice rang out from the stairs, which she had descended unnoticed.

"Willem, you will not speak to my husband so. If you ever cared for me at all, if all of your whispered promises meant anything, you will leave our home and never darken our door again."

Caspar gaped at Karin as Willem bit off whatever reply he had been tempted to make and turned on his heel. The slam of the door made Karin blink and jump, and then she was throwing herself into Caspar's arms, weeping.

Chapter 6

"We were children growing up together, and he was one of the few boys left in town after the militia's recruiters came calling," Karin explained, as the two of them sat side-by-side on the sewing table. Her tears had mostly dried, but she was still sniffling from time to time.

"We spent so much time together when we were younger that I think everyone just assumed that we would marry when we came of age. Everyone, that is, except for me. He was a friend, the brother I never had, a fellow trouble maker around the town, and nothing more."

She smiled wanly at him. "When he finally professed his love to me, and asked if he might seek Papa's permission to court me, I thought it was another of his boyish pranks."

Her expression grew more serious. "When I laughed and laughed at his wonderful joke, he turned red and called me many vile names before rushing away and returning home. I did not encounter him again at all for many months, and when I did, he acted as though he could not even see me."

She shrugged. "I missed my friend, of course, but the things he had said had so wounded me that I wanted nothing more to do with him, either. We saw each other around from time to time, of course—this is too small a town to avoid someone who lives here completely—and once he met Marysa, his attitude toward me seemed to soften somewhat."

Caspar pulled her into his side for a comforting embrace. "You broke each other's hearts, and he never forgave you for it."

She glanced up at him. "Perhaps I broke his, but mine was never at hazard. I regretted losing his friendship, but it may well be that we were never fated to remain friends, once his sympathies with the King were revealed. I wondered why he had never answered the recruiter's calls, but when I witnessed him tear down and tread upon a broadside celebrating our victory at Trenton, I came to understand."

"So you've known all along that he was a Loyalist?"

"He became much more circumspect about his views after the property confiscation acts, and I made the naïve assumption that they had caused him to reconsider his beliefs. Instead, it seems that he only became angrier. With the end of the war and its promises to restore Loyalists' property, I suppose that he no longer feels the need to disguise his sentiments."

"It explains much of what his child has said to Bjorn. Had I known that you had rejected him as a suitor, I think I would not have let our children play with Betje. A man's heart never fully heals from such a wound, even if it was delivered with no ill intent."

She gave him a sheepish look. "I did not want you to feel jealous of him, since there was truly nothing between us besides childhood friendship. I can see, though, that it was a mistake to keep that past from you, no matter how good my intentions were in doing so."

He gave her a playful squeeze. "Have you any other disappointed suitors I ought to know about?"

She giggled, and said, "Only a Rennapi prince who offered my father a fine buckskin cape for me when I was Lena's age." At his confused expression, she said, "I am fairly certain that my father made that up, if only because the Rennapi left these parts before I was born. He always said, though, before you arrived, that a man should never turn down a good offer."

Solemnly, Caspar said, "If your father desires a buckskin cape in exchange for your hand, I will gladly pay his price. I am not so skilled with leather as I should like, but I will do my best, as you are well worth it."

Karin frowned at him until he finally broke character and grinned at her. "In truth, all I can offer him is your happiness and those two imps of ours, but he seems well satisfied with those as your bride-price."

She fisted him in the side, making him jump and laugh. "The very idea that I should be bartered like a bolt of good cloth or a prized horse. Have I not any choice in the matter?"

"You may remember, my dearest, that I asked you whether I could approach your father. Once you gave your assent to that, of course, the matter was out of your hands—" He chopped off his teasing comments as he jumped away, laughing, to avoid another bruising of his ribs.

Trying to restore a serious tone, he asked, "I suppose that we have a permanent enemy in him. Do you think that Willem's opinions of me will cause our neighbors to turn against us? Have I put our business at risk by failing to be conciliatory to him?"

"I do not believe so, no. Few remain in these parts who stayed loyal to the Crown, and of those, even fewer would put their own standing in the village at risk by declaring openly for the defeated king."

"Even with the restoration of their rights and property by the treaty?"

"I cannot answer for the views of a Loyalist, since I have never been one, but I should think that they would be as circumspect as possible in this situation. There are other grounds on which to seize their property, should they make too much trouble."

Caspar made a sour face. "I think I would rather that there be fewer ways to justify taking a man's property, whether it serves to protect me in this case or not." He shrugged, then, adding, "Of course, as I own no property, I cannot vote to effect change. But that does not prevent me from thinking about it or talking with you about it."

"Papa can vote, so it might be even more effective to discuss it with him."

"Perhaps," Caspar said, but the matter seemed of less importance than the more pressing questions of avoiding the loss of business that could result from having a dedicated foe.

Karin interrupted his musings to say, "In any event, I believe that Willem's campaign of saying awful things about us in front of Betje actually has very little to do with your past, and everything to do with my past with him. There is nothing we can do about it now, other than to make sure that your customers so love your work for them they will ignore anything that Willem might insinuate about you."

She hopped down from the sewing table. "That means that I should stop distracting you from your work and let you get the next piece completed in a timely fashion, and with your usual attention to quality."

Glancing up at the roof, she added, "Not only that, but Bjorn has been quiet for far too long. I am frightened for what I will find when I go back upstairs."

Laughing, Caspar waved a hand to urge her to hurry. He stood up himself and put another log on the fire to restore some of the warmth that van Dusen had wasted, and relit the tapers before settling back down to put the finishing touches on a set of stays for the fishmonger's wife.

It had been a profitable summer for the quiet little man, and Caspar remembered the quirk of a smile on his face when he had proudly presented the price of the garment in specie, the coins ringing clearly against each other.

Finally, he spread out the finished piece on the clean surface of the sewing table, his practices eye roving over it to look for any flaws. He ran his fingertips over the stitching that ran around the ends of the lengths of whalebone, knowing that those were often the spots that failed first as the wearer moved around. The last thing he wanted was the fishmonger's stout wife coming in to complain that his work had resulted in her being uncomfortably poked when she bent to pick something up from the floor.

Satisfied, he folded the garment carefully and pulled out a length of silk cord to a suitable length, cut it, and tied it gently around the stays. That job complete, he returned to the fussy work of adding buttonholes to the waistcoat he'd been working on.

Buttonholes were his least-favorite task, especially on a thick woolen waistcoat—although a full coat was substantially worse, with its multiple layers of heavy fabric and the elaborate decorative embroidery most customers wanted around the buttons. However, the light was finally good enough that he could extinguish the candles and work by sunlight. Whatever clouds had darkened the sky that morning had cleared, and it was a clear wintry day outside.

He fetched the waistcoat from the in-progress shelf and laid it out carefully so that he could mark the buttonholes uniformly along the left front panel. His straightedge and a folded paper in hand, he bent to the work, making quick dashes and lines on the cloth with a fine pencil.

Cutting a length of thread and running its length through a notched block of beeswax, he threaded his needle and set to outline the first buttonhole with short running stitches, securing the layers of fabric together to keep the cut he'd marked aligned as he worked.

The needle darted back and forth through the cloth under his practiced hand, and he soon fell into the mindless routine of running tight, close stitches around the perimeter of the buttonhole, reinforcing it and holding the cloth steady against years of future service.

His mind wandered as he worked, considering the utility of the feature he was adding. Such a minor detail, a buttonhole, noticed only when the surrounding cloth unraveled, or the stitching gave way. Waiting on his shelf were two shirts and a pair of breeches—none of his manufacture—that needed buttonhole repairs. About the only thing less appealing to work on than sewing a new buttonhole was trying to repair an old one.

However, his apprenticeship had prepared him to deal with all such challenges with confidence and skill. His eyes, he had to admit, had been sharper then, and his fingers more nimble, but for all that the years had taken away, they had also given him more experience in where shortcuts could be taken and where they were disasters waiting to happen.

The latter was more often the case, and so he rarely took any chances with easier ways or modern innovations. His customers did not come to him with an expectation of instant satisfaction to their needs, but rather for his reputation of doing reliable, careful work, for every job, whatever its size. After the second buttonhole was complete, he looked up and noted that the light was again fading with the early onset of evening in this part of the year.

He sighed and folded the waistcoat back up after examining the two completed buttonholes closely. They were neat and consistent, and he grunted with approval at his own work before returning the piece to the shelf.

Stretching and then pressing the tightness out of each of his hands in turn, he went to the counter and flipped through the notes he had there. He would need to bring the stays over to the fishmonger in the morning, though if the sky were still clear on the morrow, he might instead see if he could instead hoard the daylight and finish the wretched buttons.

In just a few more years, Bjorn would be old enough to entrust with such duties as delivering orders around town, but for now, Caspar had to do it all alone. He sighed and set the notes in order on the counter before throwing the bolt on the door and going upstairs for the night.

Chapter 7

The shopkeeper held up the completed waistcoat with open admiration on his face. "Mister Schmidt, your work is even better than I had been led to expect. Those buttons look magnificent on it. This is a noble piece of work, sir!"

Caspar acknowledged the compliment with a faint smile and a nod of his head. "Would you like to try it on, Mister Lathrop? I will feel more sure of it once I see it on you."

"Eh? Of course, of course." The man laid the piece down on his shop counter and untied the apron from around his neck, folding it and setting it beside the new waistcoat on the countertop. Next, he worked the buttons of his shabby old waistcoat open. Peeling it off his torso, he revealed a worn and stained shirt, and Caspar made a mental note to ask him about a couple of new ones.

Slipping his arms into the new waistcoat and fastening the buttons, the shopkeeper's smile widened as we continued, "I cannot tell you what a relief it is to have a waistcoat that fits me properly at last. I bought that old one at an auction, and while it served, it was never really made for a man of my size. But this one—well, I would say that it was as if it were made for me, but of course, it was."

He raised his arms high, and bent at the waist, turning and twisting to test the fit. "Oh, that is just a wonder," he exclaimed again. "Let me fetch my purse, so that I may pay you what you are due."

He went into the back room of his shop and emerged with coins jingling in his palm. "I know you said that you could accept the paper currency of the state, but I know, too, that specie is always a better way to repay a debt one is eager to settle properly."

Caspar bowed slightly and said, "I do appreciate it indeed, sir. I should like to offer for you a discount for paying in real money."

"Oh, no," said the shopkeeper, laying the coins down on the counter before Caspar. "Were you to do that, the council might take it ill and claim that you are actually charging extra for currency. There are enough people looking to cause a good man such as yourself trouble that there is no need to go making yourself a target for their attention."

Caspar nodded his appreciation for the other man's care on his behalf, but then asked, "Have you heard of men trying to make trouble for me, then?"

The shopkeeper flushed red and stammered, "N-no, not exactly. But you know that Dutchman van Dusen, the old Loyalist. He wants to make everyone around him miserable, and in particular anyone whose loyalty he thinks is owed to the Crown."

"He has remarked to me on that subject, yes," Caspar said dryly. "A thoroughly unpleasant man, what I have known of him. But he has no foot to stand on, do you say?"

"No leg to stand on," Lathrop corrected, smiling. "No, indeed, as a man who hid his allegiances until after the peace was signed, for the safety of his own skin, I should not think that he would feel himself at liberty to say anything about another man's loyalties."

He nodded in a conciliatory manner, adding, "Yet it only seems proper to warn you he was speaking about you in exactly that manner, until I told him that such talk is unwelcome in my shop. I'll tolerate a decent range of opinion, but to assail your character was a step too far."

Caspar again nodded in gratitude, though he was seething inwardly. Did his self-appointed enemy have no standards of honorable conduct to which he felt held? Or did he harbor such envy of Caspar for having won Karin where he could not that he was blinded to the consequences of his behavior?

He shook his head to shake away the bitter thoughts that roiled about within and returned to the business at hand. He swept his payment for the waistcoat into his hand and said, "Let us set aside this unpleasant man, and permit me to ask whether I might interest you in a pair of new shirts to go with your new waistcoat."

Lathrop looked at Caspar sharply, and then a broad grin crossed his face. "You saw the state of my old shirt, did you?"

Caspar inclined his head in acknowledgment.

The man's expression was thoughtful. "I will confess to you that this waistcoat was an expense that the state of my affairs could not fully justify. With the war over, people expect things to go back to the way they were before, but the overseas trade is still in a dismal state. That paper currency of the council's does not help matters, and though I resist accepting it, the law says that I must."

Caspar said, "I have felt it in my business, as well, sir, and I must confess that it brings me some comfort to hear that it is a universal condition, and not peculiar to my work."

He gave the shopkeeper an understanding smile. "I am fortunate in that my stock does not spoil, but the style of the day does change, and a sort of cloth that had been in demand, or things like buttons depicting General Washington that everyone wants now might suddenly be only of value for melting down, should public opinion of that worthy man change."

Lathrop's mouth was still set in a thoughtful grimace. "Well, think that Missus Lathrop would appreciate me wearing something less disreputable, and I expect you will make me a good price for them. Seeing how good your finework is, I trust that your ordinary square-cut shirt can be relied upon."

He nodded briskly. "Very well, two shirts, plain, with simple thread buttons, nothing fancy, just serviceable."

Caspar bowed deeply. "It will be as you say, Mister Lathrop. I have a supply of the plain linen in my shop already. If I may take a few measurements, I can have those ready for you within the . . . fortnight? Is that the word? Before the new year, in any event."

"That will be perfectly satisfactory."

"Does three shillings apiece seem fair?"

The shopkeeper pondered for a moment, and then answered, "Two and sixpence would seem fairer."

Caspar offered his hand to settle the negotiation. Two and sixpence was the price he had originally thought to offer, but he knew from experience that he needed to leave some room for a counteroffer.

After shaking Lathrop's hand, he dug into his pocket and pulled out a pair of small scissors and a strip of paper. "Let us get you measured, sir."

On his way hope, the gray sky that had been menacing all day finally delivered on its threats, with snow beginning to fall.

When he left Lathrop's shop, it was still just a few hesitant flakes, sentinels to the rush of snow that followed. By the time he had arrived home, he could scarcely see the other side of the street, and he had to pause under the awning at his door to shake snow off his hat and cloak.

Once inside, he called up to Karin to tell her he had returned home. She answered down the stairs, "Papa is here on a visit, and I told him he may not step foot back outside until the snow has stopped, even if that means that he must sleep here tonight."

Caspar smiled to himself and answered, "Mister Jacobson, I hope that you have submitted yourself to your fate, because once your daughter has made such a proclamation, there can be no argument with her."

His father-in-law called back, laughter in his voice, "I am resigned to accepting your hospitality for as long as the weather continues to hold me here. Karin is making *pepparkakor*, so it is no hardship."

Inhaling greedily, Caspar understood now why he had felt like *Jul* was upon them. The spicy, sweet aroma of the ginger-rich biscuits brought a wide grin to his face, and he practically vaulted up the stairs.

The children sat at the table with their *morfar*, each of them contentedly munching on a biscuit. Jacobson looked up at Caspar's arrival and laughed out loud.

"One would think that you had been raised Swedish, Mister Schmidt, for how excited you are for the *pepparkakor*."

"A person does not have to have grown up with such good fortune as these children have to know that *pepparkakor* mark the darkest days of the year, and the return of the light. And, naturally, they are also delicious."

Leaning past Karin and brushing a kiss on her cheek as he did so, Caspar snatched up a biscuit from the plate where she was arranging them, earning a playful glare from her in the process. He took a bite from the crisp, thin biscuit and let its sweetness play across his tongue.

"Have I said to you today, my dear, how grateful I am to have married you?" He spun her around and soundly kissed her on each cheek, and then on the tip of her nose.

"Not more than a handful of times, husband, but you really must contain yourself in the presence of my father and the children."

Her father waved her objection away. "*Nej*, do not worry on my account. It makes me happy to see that you are so well cherished. No father could wish for more for his daughter."

"You see, dear? And the children are accustomed to it by now. If I were to stop kissing you in their presence, they would undoubtedly begin for to worry. We cannot have that, can we?"

She pushed him away playfully and turned back to her work. "You may be right, but do not let that invite you to more misbehavior. Only one more biscuit, lest you spoil your appetite for supper."

Caspar feigned surprise. "You have time for this and for supper, as well? Truly, you are a wonder."

She rolled her eyes at him over her shoulder. "Having my father here to keep the children occupied helped."

Jacobson raised a half-eaten biscuit in affirmation. "And for my service, she permits me to an extra biscuit."

Bjorn spoke up, holding aloft the remaining crescent of his biscuit. "Mama gave me an extra for keeping *morfar* occupied, and

Lena got an extra for being cute."

Caspar favored his wife with a frown. "I begin to understand. Extra biscuits for everyone else, but not for me."

She shrugged. "And what have you done that might earn you a third biscuit?"

"For the first thing, I have walked home in this storm. For the second, I was paid for that fine waistcoat today, and for the third thing, I persuaded Mister Lathrop that he ought to buy two new shirts from me."

Karin made a show of pretending to consider his case, and then said, in a mock grudging tone, "I suppose that you can be permitted one more biscuit before supper. But if you fail to clear your plate, there will be no more until tomorrow."

Bjorn laughed at seeing his father subjected to the same rules that applied to himself, and Lena, taking her cue from him, joined in with a high, merry giggle.

After they had stopped laughing, Caspar said, "Yes, Mama," playing along by adopting a bashful tone, which triggered another round of laughter from the children.

Their grandfather said, "There is entirely too much happiness in this house. I do not know how you can bear it, Mister Schmidt."

Caspar spread his hands. "Whether or not I choose to bear it will not change it, so I may as well relax and join in."

Jacobson pursed his mouth and nodded. "A wise approach, my friend." Then, squaring his shoulders and taking a deep breath, he said, "We need to talk, you and I, Mister Schmidt. There is trouble brewing that you ought be aware of."

Chapter 8

Caspar felt his blood run cold at the older man's words. For Jacobson to have chanced the weather and then to have sat and waited for his return, whatever tidings he came bearing must be grave, indeed.

He asked, "Ought we to go downstairs, so as not to disturb Karin and the children?"

His father-in-law said, "If Karin can handle these two for a little while, that might be for the best."

Karin spoke without turning away from the dough she was rolling out. "I will manage for a time. Go and have your talk."

Jacobson rose from the table and started down the stairs. His merry mood of a moment before had evaporated, and the clutch of panic in Caspar's chest gave another squeeze. He made his way down the stairs, and went to sit on his sewing table, opposite where the other man had taken up a perch on the stool.

"What is this about, Mister Jacobson?"

"Well, it seems that you have made some enemies in this town, which is a remarkable achievement for a man who does honest work and minds his own business. And yet, there is nobody who can escape having some person or another appoint themselves as their enemy."

He shrugged. "So it seems to be for you, my friend."

Caspar could feel some of the tension flow out of his

shoulders with the knowledge that this, at least, was a problem that he had already had some awareness of.

He said, "I should expect that one of them is that Dutchman, van Dusen."

Jacobson nodded. "He is, indeed, one who has spoken against you, spreading rumors you purchased cloth from a privateer during the war, using stolen goods to keep your costs down."

Caspar scoffed. "Surely nobody believes that? I did make a favorable price on some cloth that a friend bought on my behalf from a gentleman in Philadelphia. The seller was in some financial difficulty, but both he and I profited from the exchange."

"Of course, and a man of business must always avail himself of such opportunities when they arise, particularly in these hard times."

"Even so, the cloth was imported before the war began, and had suffered somewhat for the time in storage. Oh, not much of it was damaged beyond use, but there were moths, and even some rat-chewed bits. Had the gentleman disclosed those facts, I might have directed my friend to drive a harder bargain with him."

Caspar shrugged. "Still, I likely got it for half of what I would have paid elsewhere, and he did not insist on specie, so I could turn some paper currency into something that would hold its value better."

Jacobson raised a hand to stop Caspar. "As I expected, then, the rumors that van Dusen is trying to start about you should be easy enough to overcome."

He gave Caspar a curious glance. "Has Karin described her past interactions with him?"

"Yes, she told me about his failed attempt to persuade her

to let him talk to me about making a match with her. It sounded to me like a case where they misunderstood each other terribly, and it cost him dearly."

"*Ja*, and he has never forgiven her for it." Jacobson glanced toward the stairs and lowered his voice. "I learned of it when he came to me anyway and asked whether there was a suit he could make for her hand, over her objections."

He made a sour face and said, "I sent him on his way, naturally. The very idea of trying to get Karin to do something against her will is both silly and dangerous. So I don't think we need to worry much on van Dusen's account. The other party, though, may be more difficult to deal with."

The older man looked uncomfortable for a moment. "Son, I haven't inquired too deeply into how you came to be here in this village. A good man is always welcome, regardless of what he might have left behind."

Caspar frowned. "What are you getting at, Mister Jacobson?"

"There is a newcomer to town who has not very much English, but what he does have, he spends telling stories about you. He was a Hessian soldier, late of Captain Ewald's company, and he claims that you also come from that company."

Caspar nodded. "I've not spoken of it, but neither have I made any secret of it. I became separated from my company at Cooch's Bridge, and by the time I had recovered my wits, they were too far away for me to rejoin them in safety."

As he spoke, he realized for the first time that this telling of the events of that awful day was actually not inaccurate. At worst, it was slightly more charitable to his motivations that might have been justifiable.

He grinned, "You may have heard that they were cruel to anyone suspected of desertion, particularly desertion under fire. Had I returned to them, I might well have even faced the penalty of death."

Jacobson's face registered surprise, but then he nodded. "I suppose they had to maintain discipline somehow, particularly with troops who were composed of young men taken far from their homes, to fight in a war that they had no particular personal stake in."

He glanced up at Caspar. "If a man did desert from service to the Crown under such circumstances, I doubt that most here would find any fault in it."

Caspar looked away, and then shrugged. "In truth, I don't know whether I intended to desert or just fell down in an accident. It doesn't matter that very much, though, because the outcome was the same. I left the service of Captain Ewald's company and made my way to this village. I will not apologize for the path that brought me to your daughter or to the life that I have here."

"And I will not ask you to apologize for it. But you should know that this former colleague of yours seems to think that you have been keeping it a secret, and hopes to harm you by revealing it."

Caspar nodded slowly. "I met the man several weeks ago, and when he recognized me, he spoke of many hardships he had endured and which I had escaped."

Jacobson looked surprised. "So you knew he was in town?"

"I knew he had come to town, but I had hoped that after our meeting, he might have found some place without my presence to remind him of how much he had suffered." Caspar shrugged. "I suppose he decided to stay for vengeance of some sort."

His father-in-law made a dismissive gesture with his hands. "If that is the case, he is doing a poor job of even that. He seems to be drinking what money he arrived with, and though he has offered himself as a common laborer, the men who have had him in have reported that he arrives late, leaves early, and smells too much of ale."

Caspar shook his head sadly. "He was my sergeant when we served together, and while he was a hard man then, he did nothing that warranted this sort of fate. The company was taken into captivity—oh, I don't even remember exactly when it was—and it was common knowledge when I served that although captured officers would be treated decently, common soldiers could not expect even so much as reliable rations."

He sighed. "From what I saw of the man, he had missed many meals. He actually came in to get new breeches to better suit his reduced frame."

With a resigned shrug, Caspar concluded, "I do not blame him for resenting me. In his view, I did everything wrong a soldier could do, and have only reaped benefits, while he did everything right and suffered the consequences."

The older man shook his head, a bemused smile on his face. "I come here to tell you of a man who would like to destroy you, and you tell me that you understand why he would like to do so, and cannot disagree with his reasons. Mister Schmidt, you continue to astonish me."

Caspar chuckled. "Please do not mistake my understanding of the man's reasoning for a willingness to permit him to pursue his aim. I should like your advice on how best to deal with whatever threat he poses."

Jacobson considered for a moment, and then answered, "If the question arises, answering in frank honesty, as you did to me, is likely your best answer."

He fixed Caspar with an admonishing eye. "You could leave out the part where you questioned your own motives, and simply stick to the story that you were separated from your company, and it was not possible for you to rejoin them."

Caspar smiled. "Do not mistake me for a fool. I know I can unburden myself of the doubts I might harbor about myself when I speak with you. I would not give another man that same courtesy."

Jacobson bowed his head, smiling in appreciation for the trust that Caspar placed in him. "Once again, you prove yourself to be a worthy husband to my daughter. I am grateful that you know me to be a true friend, besides being the father of your wife."

"I am glad that you find me worthy. I shudder to think of how difficult you might make my life if you did not."

He grinned at his father-in-law, and continued, "I believe you are correct. Frank honesty with anyone who asks, but what of those who do not ask, but simply believe the man?"

"They would be unlikely to believe you if they hold you in so little regard that they will not even give you an opportunity to plead your case in answer to such accusations. I doubt that there are many such people in this village."

"Other than van Dusen," Caspar added quickly.

"Ah, yes, well, if those two join forces, we will have more work to do together to overcome them."

Chapter 9

Walking into church for the Christmas Eve service, Caspar settled into the familiar pew alongside Karin's parents, nodding in silent greeting to them both. Glancing around the room, he wasn't surprised to see a number of empty spots in the pews. The weather was foul, with gusty winds blowing alternating sheets of icy rain and sloppy, wet snow into their faces on the way over.

He was glad for the heavy woolen cloaks that he had made for himself and Karin. She had simply carried Lena under her cloak, and they had wrapped Bjorn in a warm blanket before setting out. Children simply grew too fast to try to keep them in well-fitting winter clothing.

For playing outside, Karin could stuff their clothes with fabric scraps for warmth, but for the Sunday walk to church, it was easier to simply cover them up. Fortunately, despite the hard times, theirs was a reasonably prosperous church, and the pastor could keep it well-warmed for services. As a result, the children were likely to nap through the sermon, though they might wake up for the hymns.

Though it differed from the services he had grown up with in Germany, and was at present in a state of some upheaval, joining Karin's congregation had been a natural choice when they had started to court. Hearing Biblical passages he knew being quoted in English helped his language skills, even as Mister Jacobson complained the sermons were better when they had been given in Swedish.

The congregation was nominally affiliated with the Swedish Lutheran church, but Caspar had heard his father-in-law engage in spirited debates over whether they ought to formalize their shift to the English Episcopal church.

It had been hard to follow, because they often shifted into Swedish when their emotions ran high, but the parts in English had been informative, to say the least.

Mister Persson had said, with heat in his tone, "Karl, the *Svenska Kyrka* has made it clear that they scarcely care about our church's maintenance any longer. Why, the archbishop in Upsalla stopped even paying for their pastors' traveling expenses any further than London, leaving us to have to raise the funds to have their representative travel the rest of the way to our shores."

Mister Jacobson had let the other man say his piece, and had then asked, calmly, "And does the Church of England offer to send us one of their pastors, now that the war is concluded? Will their man preach in praise of American independence, or sow doubt among the congregation about their wayward state in the community of the Episcopalians?"

This had been one of the moments when the conversation had shifted to Swedish, and when they returned to being calm enough to converse in English, Mister Jacobson had needled Persson, asking, "Are you just saying that because you never really wanted to see the American rebellion succeed?"

Swedish flowed again, and finally, Mister Persson had said, his tone resigned, "I shall never understand completely, my friend, why you are so completely devoted to the independence of these states from England, but the matter is not something over which I wish to make a break from you."

Jacobson nodded his agreement with the sentiment, and Persson continued, "I should like to leave the matter as simply this: I do not believe that God cares whether we address him in Swedish, German, or English, and I do not even think He is overly concerned with whether we follow the *Svenska Kyrka* liturgy or that of the Church of England."

Caspar's father-in-law looked stubborn for a moment, and then put out his hand. "We shall both know, in due time, and I confess that I do hope for the sakes of both our souls that you have the right of this."

Persson smiled and shook his friend's hand. "If not, well, then, I shall have to travel from Heaven to visit you and taunt you with the truth that has been revealed."

Jacobson guffawed and retorted, "It may be that I am the one who must beg leave of Saint Peter to spend time with an old friend, but whichever way it works out, I look forward to it."

For his part, Caspar was inwardly surprised to hear either man say such impious things, but, he reflected, he had not known either of them for that long.

Caspar had felt warmly welcomed by the congregation when he had appeared among them for the reading of the banns before his marriage to Karin. There was more singing than he was accustomed to, and the congregants were less likely to defer automatically to the pastor than was the case at home, but the changes were easy to accept when they came with the inducement of Karin as his wife.

The pastor emerged and climbed the short steps to his pulpit, interrupting Caspar's musings. In short order, between the man's tendency to adopt a monotone drone while preaching his sermon, and the warmth of the room, Caspar found himself dozing off a bit.

He was jerked back into full wakefulness by Karin and Mister Jacobson rising on either side of him to join in singing the first hymn of the service. Scrambling to his feet, he found his place in the music and added his voice to the crowd.

As he sat, he spotted a familiar face in the sparse crowd, and felt the old knot of tension between his shoulder blades tighten up again. Sergeant Graff had taken a place in a pew on the far side of the church, and looked uncomfortable and out of place. Despite himself, Caspar sympathized with the man's discomfort, remembering the first few services he had attended here.

Then he saw Graff turn to glare at him, and any sympathy he might have been harboring was replaced immediately with fear. Was this man going to denounce him publicly, relying on the strength of his testimony to convince a room full of strangers that one of their number was not who he seemed?

Caspar's mind raced. Was he prepared to respond to Graff's accusations, if they came? How would his neighbors and friends, people who had known him for six years, react to anything that Graff might have to say?

Caspar was so preoccupied with these racing thoughts he missed the cue to sit, and found himself standing alone for a moment. Karin shot him a questioning look, and her father gave him a quick glance before looking around and sighting Graff himself. Mister Jacobson grimaced, but the pastor signaled the next hymn, and all three of them were once again focused on the routine of the service.

After the recessional hymn had concluded, and the pastor had exhorted them to go in peace and serve God, Caspar again glanced over to where he'd seen Graff, and was almost as surprised to see the man missing as he had been to see him in the first place.

He turned back to his wife, who asked, "What was that all about, Caspar? You looked as though you had seen a ghost, instead of the Holy Spirit."

She grinned at her own witticism, and Caspar shook his head in mock disapproval. "No, my dear, I saw that same sergeant from my old company who had spoken to me in the shop."

Her attitude turned immediately somber. "I see. I had hoped that he would find some friendlier town in which to settle."

Her father spoke up then. "It seems that he found like-minded men here in our community, and that this has given him the encouragement he needed to make a home for himself here."

To Caspar, he said, "You will need to deal with him eventually, my friend, so that he is no longer a threat to your security here."

Karin's brows gathered in a scowl, and she spoke in a low, urgent voice. "What do you mean by that, Papa? Surely, you are not suggesting in a church, with the pastor's admonition to go in peace still echoing in the air, that my husband must kill this man."

Her father appeared to be taken aback, and beside him, her mother gasped, covering her mouth with her hand. "If I have given you some cause to believe that I might advocate for such a thing under any circumstances, let alone these, then I have failed to convey to you the quality of my character, daughter."

He shook his head in brisk negation. "No, your husband

and I have discussed the need to speak publicly about his past, before that man does so."

Karin looked abashed and her mother relaxed as she answered, "I apologize, Papa, for having given offense by my misunderstanding. I forget Caspar has unburdened himself of this past to me in private, but that he has never had cause to announce his history to our neighbors."

She glanced around at the emptying pews. "Still, I think that this is a matter that we ought to discuss elsewhere, lest someone else have a similar misunderstanding of your meaning."

Her father motioned his agreement with one hand, waving vaguely toward the door at the back of the church. He stood and helped his wife to her feet, fussing over her cloak even as she batted his hands away. "I can do for myself, Karl. I am not feeble, just old."

Karin bent and picked up Lena, who had been stretched out on the pew, sleeping. She arranged the child on her shoulder and Caspar arranged her cloak over both of them, fastening the clasp at her neck.

Beside where his sister had laid, still Bjorn sat quietly, his eyes heavily lidded in his nearness to returning to sleep himself. Karin called his name and reached out to Caspar for the boy's blanket as Bjorn stood and blinked dully. With everyone prepared for the weather outside, they moved to the back of the church, where the pastor stood to say his farewells to each of the congregants as they departed.

When Caspar reached the door, leading his family, the pastor called out to him, "I should like a word with you in private, Mister Schmidt, before you leave."

Caspar kept his face impassive, but inwardly, he felt his stomach drop as though he had fallen from the crown of a tall tree. He waved Karen and her parents along, saying, "Go ahead and get home. I will be there shortly."

Turning back to the pastor, he asked, "What service may I do for you, sir?"

The pastor looked confused, and then said, "Oh, no, I do not need your services, Mister Schmidt." He lowered his voice and leaned in closer. "There have been questions raised about your past that I hoped you might be able to clear up."

Glad for the advance warning that his father-in-law had given him of this attack, Caspar was nonetheless dismayed that the accusation had come so quickly. His confused scowl was more genuine than it might have otherwise been as a result. "Questions? What sort of questions, and by whom?"

The pastor had the grace to look uncomfortable. "When you came to our community several years ago, you were welcomed and found opportunities to make a home and a life for yourself here. Nobody inquired where you had come from, and under what circumstances."

Caspar nodded. "I am ever grateful for the kindness I found here, and appreciated that there was little more than casual curiosity about what had brought me to these shores, and then to this town."

He shrugged and added, "There is not much to tell, and it will likely come as no surprise that I came to America as a Hessian soldier, pressed into service from my home and sent here to fight against American rebels. I got separated from my company when we were ambushed, and could not find my way back. Enough time passed that I knew I would be considered a deserter if I could ever find my unit, and might even be put to death."

He gave the pastor a quick smile. "Let us say that at a certain point, it seemed wiser to start over as a new American than to try very hard to find my unit."

Nodding out through the open door, he said, "I would imagine that this question was raised by the newcomer who attended our services today. I know that man. He came to my shop a few weeks ago, and when we recognized each other, it was as I had feared. He had been my immediate superior when I was in the Hessian company under Captain Ewald, and he accused me of being a deserter and a traitor."

The pastor nodded thoughtfully. "You are correct in your presumption that it was that man who had come to me with accusations related to you conduct in the war. He claimed, besides deserting, that you had provided intelligence to the force that had ambushed your company, causing the deaths of several British troops at their hands."

He smiled grimly. "Not all of this congregation were enthusiasts for the cause of American independence, as you likely know. I worry these accusations could damage your standing among your neighbors here."

Caspar had not expected the pastor to so readily appear to take his side in the matter, but he answered steadily, "I assure you that I shared no intelligence with the American army. I was far more concerned with trying to find my company, and then with trying to *not* be found by them, but I never wished them ill. I had friends among their ranks, if nothing else."

He shook his head. "I think that my old superior may

harbor particular resentment toward me for having avoided sharing his fate of being held prisoner after our company was defeated. I am saddened, though, that he has felt it necessary to spread baseless stories about me. I have heard it said that he has taken to the bottle for comfort, and that may be clouding his judgment."

The pastor's mouth compressed into a tight line of disapproval, and then he said, "Regardless of how we may have impaired our reason, we are commanded to refrain from bearing false witness against our neighbors, and that is not a commandment that leaves much room for spreading stories one thinks might be true, because those stories make our own circumstances easier to bear."

Glancing over Caspar's shoulder at the snow now falling more thickly, he said, "I will remind our mutual acquaintance of that fact when next I see him. But now, get home before the weather gets any worse."

Chapter 10

"I cannot believe the nerve of that man, to make up wild stories about my actions after I left his service." The walk home had given Caspar time to build up a head of righteous anger. "I am no saint, but neither am I a traitor who would sell out friends to be slaughtered."

His father-in-law gave him a sympathetic look. "I cannot imagine what it must feel like to hear such accusations leveled against yourself. I am gratified, though, that the pastor seemed inclined to believe you over a stranger. It is a mark of the esteem in which you are held by this community, my friend."

Caspar frowned. "Had I not been ready to answer the accusations that Graff had made against me, I am not so certain that he would have been so fast to take my side in this matter. Indeed, I believe that the question might have hung in the balance when he asked me to speak with him. If I had evaded giving him satisfactory answers, he might have taken up the denunciation on that man's behalf."

Jacobson held his hands up, saying, "It may be as you say. But you comported yourself well, and earned his support against this Graff fellow."

"And I am grateful to you for alerting me to the hazard he presented. I should have been hard put to have answered unprepared."

"Oh, you knew he was about, from your original encounter with him. I think that you would have answered the pastor's questions well enough."

"I would have had no knowledge of reliance on strong drink to keep his demons at bay, and that may have been the argument that swayed the pastor beyond anything else I said. He may not be dedicated to abstaining from the drink, but I do not think that he approves of those who spend more time looking for the bottoms of their cups than they do the salvation of their souls."

His father-in-law laughed. "Few in his position would, it is true. But for a man who is bent on revenge, there is little satisfaction to be found in the word of God. Forgiving those who trespass against you runs counter to what this Graff fellow seems to be about."

Looking up from where she was sorting dried beans, Karin said, "What I do not see is how he can hold that Caspar has trespassed against him at all. What is there to be forgiven?"

Caspar's expression became thoughtful, and he said, "It is a very fair question, and one that that bears asking. Is it injury that he wants to redress, or simply envy?"

Karin's father said, "And if it is envy, our pastor has even less interest in intervening in the matter."

Their conversation was interrupted by the sound of someone pounding on the door downstairs. Caspar, startled, rose from the table and went downstairs to answer.

Opening the door, he found a pitiful figure huddled under a thin woolen cloak, which was soaked through from the rain that had started up again. The man's face was concealed under the hood of the cloak, but his identity was less important to Caspar than was his plight. No man should be out in this sort of weather without shelter, and protected so shabbily.

He pulled the man inside and closed the door to stop the cold draft from adding to his guest's misery. "Here, sit, and let me get the fire stoked up to warm up the room."

He urged the stranger to the stool before the fire, and turned to add kindling to the banked coals. Once he had satisfied himself that the small flames that sprang up would ignite the larger pieces of wood, he finished laying the fire and turned back to face his visitor.

He was scarcely surprised to find that it was Graff, his eyes wandering unsteadily as he huddled under the wet cloak. There was something of the man's movements that had been familiar, even under the shapeless cloak. The sour ale-house aroma the man gave off, even from a pace away, had also made him think it might be Graff. However, he could make no sense of his old commander's presence in his house.

He addressed the man in German, asking, "Sergeant Graff, what brings you to my door in such a state? When I saw you at the church, you seemed to be hale and in tolerably good spirits, whatever our differences may have been."

"Mm in spirits, at least," Graff mumbled in reply. "No place else to turn. No public house will have me, and it is too cold to stay out of doors. The spirits I could find warmed me for a while, but I've seen men . . . men . . . eh, yes, freeze to death after warming themselves so. Only man I could think of who knows me in this place, and he's the one who left me to rot in captiv . . . captivity, but coming to you is better than dying before the sun rises again."

Caspar regarded the man, and then said quietly, "You spoke to the pastor about me, and told him things that were not true, things that could have cost me dearly within my community, had they been believed without consideration. We may disagree over whether or not I deserted the company, but that does not give you leave to spread rumors that I furthermore betrayed them to the Americans by providing intelligence. I may have been shy, sir, but I am no traitor."

He pursed his lips, seeing Graff's blank look. Whatever human intelligence had once animated those eyes was—for the moment, at least—absent. As he looked at the man, a thin line of drool dripped from one corner of his mouth, and Caspar had to look away in disgust. He knew that the man had suffered, and had done what he could to disrupt Caspar's like here, but to see him so debased was unbearable.

What was his responsibility to a man who had sought to destroy him? How was he to treat this foe, suddenly turned helpless, self-destructive, and needy? He had gotten the man out of the weather, but could he turn his enemy back out to his fate?

Caspar remembered suddenly the conversation he'd just been having with his father-in-law. This man had certainly trespassed against him, but the commandment was clear and uncompromising. He owed this man the same compassion and care that he would owe any fellow human being. Their differences could wait to be settled on another day. For tonight, survival was something that Caspar could offer Sergeant Graff.

He sighed and rose from where he'd crouched beside the fire, pulling down an old, coarse, but dry woolen blanket from his shelves. Unfastening the soaked cloak from Graff's neck, he could not help noticing how the man's neckbones protruded at the top of his spine. He wrapped the dry blanket around the man's spare form and led him over to lie on on the floor near the fire to dry off and warm up. By the time Caspar reached the stairs to go back up and tell his family what had happened, Graff was already snoring audibly.

Chapter 11

Ful morning dawned crisp and bright, the prior day's storm having lifted. What had been shifting back and forth between rain and snow had turned definitively to snow, and the town lay under a thick, blinding blanket of white. Caspar had risen early, slipping out of bed quietly so as to avoid disturbing Karin.

Descending the stairs, he found Graff in the same position as when he had gone up the night before, with the cat curled up atop him. He suffered a momentary panic of wondering if the man had died in the night, after all.

However, at the sound of the bottom tread on the stairs squeaking under Caspar's weight, he snorted and rolled over, and Caspar tried to calm his galloping heartbeat as he approached the man. The cat jumped down as he turned and stalked off, looking offended.

Once again, Caspar was struck by the overwhelming smell of sour alcohol that surrounded Graff, and he wondered just where the man had found the money to buy enough liquor to have polluted himself so severely. As he got closer, his nose detected that his guest had also soiled himself in the night.

Sighing, he sat on the stool in front of Graff and waited for the man to wake up. They had matters to discuss. The drunkard rolled away from him and started snoring again, and Caspar had

had enough. He nudged Graff with the point of his shoe.

"Wake up, Mister Graff," he said, again using German so that there could be no possibility of misunderstanding each other. The man groaned and pulled the blanket closer around himself. Looking at it more closely, Caspar frowned. The man was not wrapped in the same coarse woolen blanket that he had but on him the night before, but a fine, embroidered blanket that a customer had brought to him for a patch.

He scowled, his goodwill evaporating. He barked, "Private Graff, show a leg!"

The man gave a surprised grunt and blearily rose to his feet, both blankets puddling around him. He peered at Caspar, confused, and then scowled and said, "I'm no private, and you have no call to speak to me in such a manner."

"You are correct, mister, that you are no private. Even a private would know better than to so incapacitate himself that he could not find his way to the privies."

He pointed to the fine blanket, which had a visible yellow stain on it. "And no private would steal a blanket from his host, doing permanent damage to it."

Graff had the decency to look abashed at that, but he recovered himself in a moment. Despite his level of intoxication the prior night, he was waking up relatively quickly now, reminding Caspar of a man he'd known during his apprenticeship, who had been in the process of drinking himself to death. Like Graff, that man had been able to give the appearance of sobriety even while he was still under the influence of spirit sufficient to have left most men flat on the floor.

Graff pulled himself up to his full height, saying, "I do not know how I came to be in your house, Herr Schmidt, and if I am indeed your guest, then I will offer apologies for the damage I have done."

He looked around the room suspiciously. "How did I find myself sleeping on the floor of your shop, rather than at my inn, in my bed?"

"You presented yourself to my door late in the night, soaked to the skin and you told me you had lost your lodgings. You were in the grip of whatever spirits you drank last night, and I could see that you were within an hour of freezing to death. Whatever our differences have been, I cannot send any man to such a fate."

Graff frowned sourly and answered, "It seems, then, that I am in your debt for my life."

Caspar made a dismissive gesture with one hand. "I do not keep such debts on my ledger. Nor will I turn a guest out unfed into such conditions, particularly on Christmas morning."

When he'd gone back upstairs the prior night and told his amazed family what the disturbance had been, Karin had initially advocated for sending the drunkard out to his fate. She was still so incensed at the difficulties he had threatened to expose Caspar to.

Her father had said, in a soothing, reasonable tone, "Karin, my dear, I have never known you to be so bitter and unforgiving. Perhaps this man found his way to your door so that you and your husband might show him he was wrong about the events of the past."

Karin had harrumphed and crossed her arms, but before everyone had settled down to sleep, she had agreed that Graff would be offered a civil *Jul* breakfast.

By that time, the *vitergröt* was already simmering over the huge *Jul logg* in the kitchen hearth, hoarded barley and precious late-season milk combining to make the traditional meal to start the day of *Jul.*

Karins' mother remarked, "Back home, my *mormor* told me they might serve the *vitergröt* with a splash of small ale to sweeten it, but my *morfar* found he preferred a dollop of molasses along with a generous knob of butter."

Caspar smiled and said, "I like the molasses and butter well enough, myself, but I might try it with the ale sometime. However, if we are to share it with my unexpected guest, I should rather maintain the new family tradition."

Karin gave the large pot a stir, saying, "It is a good thing that there is enough in here to last the family until *trettondagsafton,*" which Caspar knew was well after the start of the new year. "One more bowl tomorrow will not matter that much, I suppose."

Bjorn sat up from where he had been pretending to sleep. "I am glad that you are not sending that man out when the julbock is looking for someone to butt someone with his horns."

Karin sighed and said, "The *julbock* prefers to come for little boys who will not sleep on *Jul.*"

Bjorn's eyes opened wide, and then he screwed them shut and threw himself back down onto his bed, snoring in an enthusiastic mimicry of sleep.

Karin's mother smiled gently and said, quietly, "I remember telling you the same thing when you were a little girl, but you were hardly so eager to convince me that you were asleep."

Karin smiled back and said, "That was because I had designs on riding the *julbock.* I just knew that if I could stay awake long enough, I could catch the old goat."

Her father grinned. "That's my daughter." Looking out through the dark windows, he added, "I think that we should all get to bed now, though. Tomorrow morning will be an early one, I am sure."

While Caspar appreciated his wife's family's traditions around the Christmas holiday, and many of them were reminiscent of what he recalled from his childhood, he could not convince her they should cut down a fir tree and bring it indoors to decorate with apples and sweets. She said only that it sounded like it would make a terrible mess in her house, and seemed like a waste of a perfectly nice tree.

When he had persisted in needling her by mentioning to her that prosperous families in his childhood home town had the added practice of placing candles in the tree to light up the darkness of the season, she had thrown up her hands. "No, no, a thousand times no. We will not be burning down our house to remind you of your childhood." He had laughed in reply, and had let the matter lie.

Two years back, Caspar had been delighted to find some smuggled frankincense on a trip to Philadelphia, and he had added a tiny nodule of it to the fireplace in his shop each of the twelve nights of Christmas. His grandmother had said that it kept the demons at bay, but he just associated it with the scents of the season.

Karin had complained about the strange smoke aroma from whatever wood he'd used, but when he had explained, she had wrinkled her nose slightly and said, "I suppose it is not so bad, now that I know it is purposeful. But don't put it in my hearth upstairs, else it will make the food taste strange."

Now, Graff looked at him sharply at the mention of Christmas. "Is it truly *Weihnachten?* The dates have lost any meaning since our company was captured. There were the warm months and the cold months, but no holidays or other occasions to mark the exact date. I had gotten out of the habit of paying attention to the calendar."

"Surely you heard the pastor speak of Christmas?"

"It was all in English, and my command of that language is not what I could wish it to be."

Caspar nodded. "It took me several years to understand enough to follow the services, and I remember how confusing they were when I first attended."

Graff looked at him with growing wonder on his face. "You speak to me as though I were a friend, and invite me to your table, after keeping me safe through the night. Yet I have been no sort of friend to you."

Caspar chuckled. "Too well I know it, Mister Graff. Do not mistake the hospitality offered to a guest, even an unexpected and unwelcome one, for the hand of friendship."

Graff's eyes narrowed. "Very well. I will not forget either the hospitality or the fact that I am only tolerated."

Caspar said, "There has been much done and said between us that would need to be corrected for that to change."

Graff spat back, "You presume, Herr Schmidt, that I have anything that I feel I need to correct." He glanced out through the shop windows to the snow-covered scene outside. "I will admit the necessity of sharing breakfast with you this morning, but I will stay under your room not one minute longer than I must."

"That suits my purposes as well, Herr Graff. Would you wait downstairs until my family is ready to break our fast together?"

Graff said nothing, but only stooped to retrieve the soiled blankets from the floor, wrapped them around himself, and sat on the stool, staring sullenly into the fire.

As Caspar climbed the stairs, he reflected on how he seemed now to hold the whip hand in dealing with Graff. Where the man had once intimidated him, had caused him to feel anxiety for his future, now he could only summon pity and disgust in thinking about him.

Moreover, it appeared Graff accepted this change in their status relative to one another. If it was disquieting for Caspar, he could only imagine how it felt to find oneself so diminished. A bitter draught to swallow, particularly for a man so proud as his former sergeant had once been.

Upstairs, Caspar found Karin out of bed, stirring the porridge and still looking bleary. Caspar looked around, and saw her parents still sound asleep on one pallet and the children sprawled out on the other. Quietly, he asked, "Did my voice wake you from downstairs? I was trying to be quiet, but the villain soiled not only the blanket I provided him, but also Missus Graham's good embroidered blanket."

Karin shook her head and whispered, "No, you know I can rarely sleep through you leaving the bed." She frowned, and added, "I have looked outside, and I find that I must agree that you were correct not to send him outside to be found when the snow melts. But what is this about Missus Graham's blanket?"

Caspar explained what had happened, and Karin's nose wrinkled in disgust. She muttered under her breath, "*Smutsigt gammal fyllo.* No good comes from those who cannot stay out of the bottle."

Her father called out in a low voice, "He may be a dirty old drunk, my daughter, but he is a guest under your husband's roof. It is better not to use such words, even when you alone can understand them."

"Papa, did you hear what he did?"

"*Nej*, but even if he drowned the fire with night water, there would be no cause to call him that."

"He drowned a customer's blanket instead," Caspar interjected. "I think it's fair to call him a dirty old drunk."

Mister Jacobson harumphed and rolled back over to face away from the hearth, and Karin smiled fondly at her father's back.

Bjorn rolled over on his pallet, his arm coming to rest on top of Lena's face, and in the wake of her struggles to push his arm away, both of the children were wide awake, grumpy, and loudly demanding that their mother to sort out who was to blame for both states.

Karin yawned and picked the baby up, settling the matter, and said to Caspar, "You may as well invite our guest upstairs to break his fast. Even a *smutsigt gammal fyllo* must be offered the *Jul* porridge at the table."

Chapter 12

Graff peered suspiciously down at the bowl of porridge as Karin placed it before him. In German, he asked Caspar, "What is this?"

Caspar answered, "It is a traditional Swedish breakfast for Christmas morning, made with barley and milk. It is quite good, though I do not remember my mother making anything quite like it in Hesse when I was a child."

The other man's expression remained wary as he lifted a spoonful of the porridge up to smell it, and then tasted a tiny sample from the end of the spoon.

Immediately, he roared, "Why did you not warn me that it was hot?"

Caspar said brusquely, "Even the children can see that it is hot from the steam that rises from it. It is not the responsibility of others to warn you of every hazard in the world."

Turning to Karin, he explained, "Our guest has apparently never mastered the art of eating a hot porridge." He made a sour face, and she frowned in an expression that told Caspar that he would be hearing more about his guest's poor manners later.

Meanwhile, Graff had cooled the spoonful enough by blowing on it that he could sample it again. He looked skeptical for a moment, then shrugged and finished the spoonful.

Bjorn was watching the whole performance with wide

eyes, and as Graff dug into his bowl for another spoonful, the boy asked, "Papa, why does the dirty man make such faces?"

Karin choked on the spoonful of porridge she had just taken, and coughed heartily. Caspar pounded on her back to help her, and when she was able to speak again, Karin said, "Bjorn, that was quite rude. You should apologize to Mister Graff."

Dutifully, Bjorn piped, "I'm sorry Mister Graff" without any inflection or pause between the words. The Hessian did not seem to register that he'd even been addressed, but was focused on emptying his bowl as quickly as possible.

Caspar said, "Bjorn, he is trying the *vitergröt* for the first time in his life. It is a strange dish to someone who has never had it before."

Bjorn seemed satisfied with this answer and returned to eating his own breakfast, until, with a shout of triumph, he spat a small, brown bean into his hand.

"I have found the bean, Mama! I will have good luck in the new year!"

Karin sighed and said, "Yes, Bjorn, you will have all of the luck for the next year."

Graff had finished his porridge by this time, and was glancing surreptitiously back toward the kitchen, but Caspar's hospitality had already been stretched to the breaking point. He said, "Herr Graff, I think it is time that you make your way back to your lodgings."

The man looked disappointed, but Karin had said that her tolerance extended no further than a single bowl of porridge. The man had been given that, and Caspar was not feeling particularly kindly toward him.

The sour reek he gave off had made the meal challenging for everyone to enjoy fully, and Bjorn had given voice to the thoughts that Caspar guessed everyone in the family had been harboring.

He stood, and Graff followed suit with evident reluctance. "I will see our guest to the door," Caspar said to Karin, and led the way to the stairs.

Down in the shop as they approached the front door, Graff turned suddenly. "Do you hate Hesse so much?"

Caspar scowled and replied, "I have no reason to love it, but neither do I hate it. What brings you to ask such a question?"

Graff looked around the shop, his old judgmental nature reasserting itself. "I can catch the smell of your frankincense, but only just barely. I see no other sign you are observing *Weihnachten* at all, but only your wife's Swedish *Jul*. Have you forgotten your home so easily as you did your company? Is there anything that you have not abandoned and betrayed?"

Caspar gaped at the man, and then answered in a cold fury, "You have never loved anything but yourself, I can see. It makes my wife happy to follow the ways of her parents, and it does me no harm. Her joy takes nothing away from me."

He shook his head slowly. "I have no other particular memories of joy in this season as a boy, *Herr* Graff. It is in her traditions that I have found some means of getting through these dark days of the season."

Graff retorted, "This land may offer nothing like the *Christkindlesmarkt*, and the foods we enjoyed as a boy cannot be readily gotten here, but you could at least be teaching your children the language of your childhood, and acquainting them with the ways of our forefathers."

"Tell me, *Herr* Graff, why did you not return home with your company when you were released?"

The man said flatly, "There is nothing there for me now, and having taken part in the contest for control of this country, I felt that the least it could grant me was a new start. I am not so foolish that I cannot see the riches that this continent offers to a man who will take what he needs from it."

Caspar said, gently, "Your reasons for staying here are not so very different from my own, save that I have furthermore had the great fortune to have found a worthy wife here, as well."

Graff scoffed, "You have been unmanned by your wife, *Herr* Schmidt, though I should not have been surprised to find it so. After all, a true man would never have abandoned the men who had stood by his side, ready to lay down their lives for one another, not knowing that there stood among them one who would fall short of that ideal."

Caspar shot back, "You don't know what happened that day, *Herr* Graff. You have never asked me how I came to be separated from our company, nor what lengths I went to in my attempts to restore myself to your service." Caspar knew he was re-writing his history now to better match the story he had been telling his father-in-law and pastor, but he was past caring to tell this man the truth.

Graff saw through him, though, it seemed, as he answered, "You may tell yourself and your family whatever stories will help you all sleep better at night, but you and I know what actually happened that day. You ran when the first shots were fired, and kept running until you could tell the rebels of our plans. You are a traitor, and no sort of man at all."

Caspar's hand shot out, striking the other man full upon the face, and jerking his head hard to the side with the impact.

Graff stood there for a long moment, stunned at the blow, and then smiled slowly. "It seems that I have hit upon some truths that are too uncomfortable for you to bear, *Herr* Schmidt." He shrugged, and added, "It is no affair of mine any more, I suppose. The war is over, and you and I are but fellow citizens of this new country. But I am glad that I know your nature."

He opened the door and smirked over his shoulder as he stepped into the drifted snow outside. "I shall be certain that our neighbors also know that you are not a man to be trusted, and barely a man at all, at that."

Chapter 13

Missus Nygard was apologetic, but firm. "I know that you have already begun drawing up the pattern, but we have had to take on unexpected expenses, and my husband told me that I had no choice but to cancel the order with you. I am sorry."

Caspar's mouth was a grim, straight line, and it took him a moment to be able to answer in a civil tone. "You were one of my first regular customers when I opened my shop, Missus Nygard, and I have always offered you the fairest prices I could afford to. Was there something lacking in the last skirt I made for you?"

She flushed slightly, and something made Caspar think that it was because she was not accustomed to lying so openly. "The quality of your work has never been in question, Mister Schmidt. You must know how terribly expensive everything has become. My husband tried to explain to me that the trade has continued to be interrupted despite the peace, and I must confess that I did not completely understand it, but he was quite firm that I must not spend money on clothing at this time."

Caspar took a deep breath and willed himself to stay calm. "Very well, Missus Nygard, but as you said, I have already done work on this order, and I have spent money to prepare to make your new gown. I did not have enough of the linen in your color for it, and had to order more from Philadelphia."

"Can you not return it, as you have not yet begun to cut the pieces for the gown?"

He shook his head in sharp negation. "That is not the way that the cloth merchants operate, no. The point of the matter is that it is impossible for me to return the deposit you made in advance of delivery."

Her brow gathered in apparent worry, which gave way instantly to anger. Primly, she said, "Mister Nygard will be around to speak to you of this, in that case. Good day to you, sir."

With this pronouncement, she whirled and left, closing the door firmly behind herself. Caspar sighed and slumped against the counter. She was the third customer since *Jul* to cancel an order, and all had come from the Swedish part of the community.

He was quite certain that Graff's Swedish was no better than his English, and very few of the Swedes spoke German, so his foe must have found some intermediary to spread poisonous rumors against him. Willem van Dusen had no Swedish, so it could not have been him. It must have been someone in the congregation at the church, someone who had reason to wish his family ill, and who spoke at least enough German to learn of Graff's wild accusations.

Sighing, he trudged up the stairs to tell Karin of this latest blow to their business. Instead of a relatively prosperous month, these canceled orders meant that they would have to rely more on beans and less on meat in the weeks ahead.

"Another one," he said without preamble. "That fine green linen gown that Missus Nygard had ordered. She was quite cross when I told her that the deposit is already spent on cloth, and threatened to send her husband around to make me give the money back."

Karin said nothing, but only grimaced and kept stirring a pot while balancing Lena on one hip.

He continued, "I cannot think of who is passing around whatever rumors are causing our neighbors to turn against us. I mean to say that while Herr Graff is obviously the origin of them, he lacks the means to overcome the barriers of language and unfamiliarity in the pursuit of his vengeance against me."

Karin cocked her head to one side and asked, "Do you suppose he is lodging with the Widow Berquist?"

Caspar scowled. "He didn't say, although he mentioned that his prior landlord had turned him out for his drunkenness. Widow Berquist would be none too fussy about such weaknesses, and only too glad for the boarder, whatever his condition."

His wife nodded, shifting Lena from one hip to the other. "Stop pulling mama's hair, Lena," she chided the toddler, who giggled and stuffed a hank of her mother's hair into her mouth.

"I think that I may have heard the woman say that she had grown up in Lübeck, which would have given her German, before she married Ole and the two of them came here."

Caspar made a sour face. "It is hard to see what Ole saw in her, but he was stuck in the old ways and would have made her learn Swedish. Strange that you never mentioned that she might have some German when you and I were trying to make ourselves understood after we met."

She smiled, answering, "We always seemed to make our desires known to one another."

"True enough. But now, why would the Widow Berquist want to cause us trouble?"

Karin looked abashed. "I may have given her cause earlier

this summer. She was at the market, negotiating for a likely-looking boar pig, and I made an unkind comment about it being a strange companion and a poorly-behaved housemate. She has not spoken to me since then."

Caspar groaned. "What prompted you to make such a remark to her?"

Karin shrugged. "There was something of a resemblance between the two in the face, and it just occurred to me. I did not expect that she might take it so ill that she would try to bring about the downfall of your business, though."

Caspar held back the answer he was tempted to make, but said only, "I am glad enough at least to have an explanation that permits me to make sense of why we are being so targeted, and through whom. Knowing this, I can now take some action to counter it."

"What will you do?"

"What I should have done as soon as Graff came to town, and most certainly after he appeared at the church."

He pursed his mouth. "I must wonder, though, whether it was Graff's tales of my desertion or his claim that I must have betrayed the company to the Americans that has aroused the most ire. I know that not everyone in the congregation was enthusiastic about the American cause, and it occurs to me that some of those may see Graff's accusations against me as an excuse to strike a blow against the rebellion."

"Even though the war is over? I would have thought that everyone was weary of the conflict, and as eager as we were to see it settled at last."

"Some stories that I learned about from the soldiers in my

company made me think many wars find their roots in the last war, rather than any fresh insult. Oh, there might be some pretense, but the reason for the pretense is that one side or the other was not satisfied with the peace, and sought to try again to accomplish their goals."

"You don't think that the Loyalists would try to start the war again?" Karin sounded frightened at the prospect.

"No, I don't think that there are enough of them left, nor have those few enough influence, but that does not mean that they might not make trouble for those of us who they hold especially responsible."

"You are no more responsible for the outcome of the war than is your cat."

Caspar smiled. "That may be, but Loyalists cannot reach General Washington or the Marquis Lafayette, but they can reach us."

"Marquis *de* Lafayette," Karin corrected automatically, adding, "At least, that is how the newspapers refer to him. It is some French term I don't understand."

He smiled at her. "It has been a while since you've felt the need to correct my English, and it turns out to have been French? That scarcely seems fair, my dear."

She smiled back, and seemed about to add something more when Lena stirred and demanded something of her mother.

"If French is difficult for me, Lena's babbling is utterly impossible to understand," Caspar laughed.

Mother and daughter turned to look at him in unison, with nearly identical expressions of disapproval, and Caspar had to laugh all the harder.

Quieting the baby by offering her a breast to suckle at, Karin asked, "What is it that you have in mind to do?"

He sighed. "I have convinced myself that it is probably useless, but what I had thought to do was simply stand before the congregation and give them the same plain truth that I shared with your father and the pastor. However, if there are people who want to misuse me in the place of the Congress or General Washington, doing that will only confirm them in their determination to do us harm."

Karin thought for a moment, absently stroking the baby's head, and then asked, "Might it be more difficult for them to pretend that they are each acting independently, or that their acts amount to some sort of coincidence, if you describe it publicly?"

"It might," Caspar replied thoughtfully, "but it might also embolden others to act, if they have not actually acted in cooperation with each other."

Karin grimaced. "Do you truly think that there are people among our neighbors who harbor such resentment in their hearts over the outcome of the recent contest that they would act openly to injure a trusted member of their community, over a matter in which you had only the most remote influence?"

Caspar shook his head sadly. "We may yet find out the answer to that question."

Chapter 14

Caspar sat in his familiar, comfortable cross-legged position upon the sewing table, his needle working steadily along a seam in yet another set of stays. These were for Miss Martyn, whose mother had brought her in for measurements just after the beginning of the new year.

As usual, for propriety, he had Missus Martyn actually take the measurements behind a screen. Miss Martyn, a giggly young woman not quite yet of marriageable age, had said that her mother's hands were tickling her during some of the measurements, but had tolerated the procedure in good grace otherwise.

When it was done, and her daughter was dressing behind the screen, Missus Martyn had handed Caspar the notched strips of paper with the measurements he needed to design the garment and said, "That Willem van Dusen has been saying some scandalous things."

Caspar froze and asked, cautiously, "What sort of things?"

"He has really been discrediting himself among those of us who are relieved that this entire war is done, and with a happy outcome. Personally, I have always known that he was not a reliable patriot, but the things he has said in the past few weeks have put him quite outside of the company of decent people."

"I am sorry to hear that," Caspar said, his heart starting to beat again. He paused briefly to consider whether to continue, and then ventured, "Our children had played together until recently, when it became clear that he was teaching his daughter to believe many ugly things."

Missus Martyn's disapproval was evident on her face. "It is bad enough when a man turns against his neighbors, but to teach his children to do likewise is quite terrible. I mentioned him to you, though, not to gossip, but to explain why, though I can make stays for my daughter myself, I had decided to bring the work to you."

Caspar's eyebrows rose. "Oh? How is that? I am always happy for new business, but I don't see a natural connection between his political persuasions and your patronage."

"Why, I thought it was perfectly obvious. He has been trying to convince people they should not give you business, as you are a notorious patriot who has turned his back on not only the English king, but your own sovereign as well. That poor Hessian soldier, recently released from captivity by the treaty, has fallen in with him, and the two of them together have been trying to make trouble for anyone who helped to secure our independence."

Caspar was not surprised that van Dusen and Graff had found each other, but he was a bit taken aback to hear himself described as having contributed to the American cause. He said, mildly, "I have not acted in particular to bring about the independence. I left such matters behind long ago."

"Oh, yes, when you deserted from the Hessian company. They have told everyone who would listen all about that. Well, that is, Willem has told everyone—that Hessian has very little to say. They have also spoken about how you revealed the Hessian company to our men defending the bridge by Cooch's tavern, which I think was a wonderfully brave thing to do."

Caspar's head spun from the revelation that the rumormongering by van Dusen and Graff had apparently produced the opposite effect from their intentions. However, all he said was, "Missus Martyn, you are too kind. I did only what any man would have under the circumstances, and while I am grateful for your patronage, I hasten to add that I am no sort of hero."

"Oh, nonsense. The penalty for desertion or informing was death, and yet you stood up for our liberty fearlessly." She patted his cheek, adding, "I am very glad to give you my business, and I know I am not alone in this sentiment. You may expect to hear from other grateful members of the community."

Finishing up the seam and trimming the end of the thread closely to the expensive silk fabric Missus Martyn had chosen on her daughter's behalf, Caspar reflected on the divide that seemed to be appearing within the community.

It was strange that people who had kept quiet about their convictions for years would only now, with the conflict settled, stir up sentiments for or against independence. While the matter was still in question, he could understand neighbors preferring to withhold their business from those on the other side of it from themselves. Likewise, he could see the reason behind going out of one's way to do business with men whose politics were agreeable.

To do so now, though, made little sense to him. He had never been particularly attached to one position or the other. If the British had prevailed against the rebellion, it might have made his position in one of her colonies more precarious, officially speaking, but on a practical level, it would have meant only minor differences in taxes.

Laws imposed by Parliament from London were of little

more personal import than laws imposed by the Congress in Philadelphia or Princeton, or wherever they were meeting now. He could not vote for either, as he owned no land, nor had he accumulated any wealth.

It was natural, Caspar supposed, for people to yearn for the days before the war, when it seemed as though any man with sufficient application of his energy could come to own property, but it seemed inevitable that the return of peace would restore that likelihood of prosperity quickly enough.

But even nostalgia for the times before the conflict had erupted seemed a poor reason to turn against one's neighbors and friends, yet he was seeing it among both the congregation at the Swedish church and in the Dutch community.

In any event, he was grateful that Missus Martyn had brought her daughter in for a set of stays, and more grateful yet that she had seemed determined to spend as much as she reasonably could on them. He still wasn't completely comfortable with her doing so based on considering him to be a hero to the patriot cause, but her commission had helped to offset the canceled work from the other side of the divide.

He considered whether to start stitching the next seam, but decided that the daylight was fading too quickly, and he was reluctant to light more tapers, literally burning money for the sake of more time to work. There was no specific deadline for the commission—"Oh, whenever you finish it; I trust your work, sir," Missus Martyn had said—and though he was charging a premium for the fine materials she had selected, he still figured his time at a modest rate. Not enough to pay for extra candles unless the work were urgent.

As he folded up the work in progress and stood to stretch, the cat suddenly dashed across the room from where he had been lazing by the hearth, and ran under his sewing table. A moment later, a high-pitched squeak demonstrated he was earning his keep, and Caspar smiled as he proudly carried his catch back to the fireside.

One less mouse to menace his supplies and work was always a good thing, and the cat was good about keeping the results of his hunting well to himself. He recalled with a wry smile that his old master, Herr Drehnbacher, had briefly kept a cat who liked to bring his kills up into the shelves to dispatch. Nobody wanted clothes that came with small, mysterious bloodstains already upon them, and so that tomcat had been encouraged to find a new home.

He bolted the door and looked out the window for a minute, contemplating the dreary, muddy scene without. The snow of the previous fortnight had melted away, leaving the streets rutted and hazardous under a sullen gray sky. Winter had never been his favorite season, but he knew that it was necessary to make ready the promise of a new spring.

Mounting the stairs slowly, he looked back at his tidy shop with a sense of satisfaction, and realized that Missus Martyn's visit had restored his optimism about the future of his venture. While it might yet be some time before he could afford to take on an apprentice—perhaps not even any sooner than when Bjorn was ready to take up the trade—he had confidence that he could continue to earn enough to keep his family comfortable, even without the business from those who wanted to use him to make some sort of point about American independence.

Chapter 15

After picking their way through the rutted muck of the streets to church, Caspar was happy that his family seemed to have brought no more mud into their pews than anyone else. After the relative happiness of the first *Jul* observation in a United States of America that had been legitimized and recognized by its former wartime adversaries and allies alike, the muddy, gray chill of the new year reflected the realities of independence.

Pastor Lundqvist's demeanor as he came to the pulpit matched the mood of his congregation, and after the hymns and routine opening prayers, his voice sounded weary as he began his sermon.

"Although we are gathered here in a time of new beginnings, it seems as though some of us are not yet ready to release our old conflicts. I would like to remind each of you of the admonition that God gave us to look always for the possibilities and benefits to be found in reconciliation."

He looked around the congregation, and Caspar's glance automatically followed where the pastor was gazing. While Graff had not returned to the church since the *Jul* service, he thought that the pastor's eye might have rested a touch longer on Missus Nygard than on some of the other members of the congregation.

The pastor went on to preach from Paul's second letter to the Corinthians, building his argument on God's urging followers of Christ to do as the Son had done, and abandon resentment about trespasses against them to reconcile with their foes.

His heart did not seem to be in the sermon, though, and Caspar wondered what could have so discouraged him. After the service had ended, and the family was making its way back home through the muddy roads, he found he was not alone in his observations.

"I wonder what was the matter with the pastor," Karin said. "His sermon seemed perfectly timely and relevant to our own problems, but other than generally reminding us that the example of Christ is to forsake holding on to resentments, he did not seem to have much specific guidance to offer."

Caspar pondered for a moment, and then answered, "I wonder if he has been hearing from people within the congregation on opposite sides of the division between those who are happy that the war is finally over, and those whose hopes have been wrecked by the peace. Despite what he said about us being subject to a commandment to reconcile with our enemies, putting that ideal into practice is a challenge even in small things, never mind the larger questions raised in a moment such as this."

"Then why did he bring it up at all, if he doesn't have any persuasive answers?"

Caspar turned and smiled at his wife. "Perhaps he hoped that by bringing it to our attention, he could start people thinking about letting go of their resentments. There is not always a single, simple answer to such difficult questions, but it can be useful to force people to confront the fact that the questions exist."

He gave her a wry smile. "I don't know if you noticed, but he seemed to give Missus Nygard his particular attention when he mentioned the importance of not holding on to our differences."

Karin chuckled. "I shouldn't wonder but that she brought her rumors to him herself, and that this was his answer to her, in as public a means as he could think of to deliver it."

Caspar nodded noncommittally. "It could be, but she is not the only one who might benefit from such an admonishment. I cannot think that it was meant for the patriot side, though, as I have not heard of any such coordinated action being taken against former Loyalists."

"You told me that the treaty called for the Loyalists to be given back their possessions, among other things. Has that been happening?"

Caspar shrugged. "I do not know for certain, but it would be a provocation if it were not, for certain. Perhaps that is where the trouble has started."

Karin grimaced. "Based upon what you told me of Mister van Dusen's comments to you, it seems as though that would be only an excuse for what they wanted to do, anyway. There does not seem to be a question of principle at work here, but merely an attempt to justify taking action against anyone that they perceive to have been aligned with the victors."

"It is a peculiar way to respond to the peace," Caspar agreed. "We have a chance to build the world anew, without the threat of fresh outbreaks of violence, and they cannot seem to accept that."

"It may also be that they are simply worried about a future that does not look to them to be as promising as the past." From behind them came the answering voice, and both of them spun around to see the pastor hurrying along to catch up with them.

Karin exclaimed, "Pastor Lundqvist! What brings you to

chase us on the street?"

Lengthening his stride further, heedless of the mud spattering the hem of his robes, he answered, "I should like very much to speak to your husband, Missus Schmidt, that is what."

Caspar answered nervously, "Of course. Shall we go to my shop, so that we can do so in warmth and comfort?"

"That would be ideal, yes, and it will permit us to speak our minds without being concerned that some passing person will hear us." He smiled quickly, but his face immediately returned to a serious, worried expression.

Caspar said nothing, but showed the way with a wave of his hand. Beside him, Bjorn looked up at the pastor with an expression of wonder on his round face.

In a high, querulous voice, he asked, "Is God coming to our house, Papa?"

The pastor laughed openly, seeming to be grateful for the opportunity for mirth, and shook his head. "No, Master Schmidt, merely a man who presumes to speak sometimes on His behalf. If I were God, perhaps I could do more good than seems possible for me in the present moment."

Bjorn seemed to accept this, and continued to trudge along on sturdy, short legs, his pantaloons gathered well above his knees to avoid the mud. His hose were hopelessly stained, but at least they were easy enough for Karin to wash. After a few more steps, he looked up at Pastor Lundqvist and asked, "If you are not God, does God at least talk to you?"

The pastor smiled and said, "Sometimes I think He does, yes."

"Does God see everything?"

The pastor nodded emphatically. "The Bible tells us that not even a sparrow may fall without Him noticing it."

"Does God tell you everything that He sees?"

Caspar grinned at his son and shared a private smile with the pastor.

Pastor Lundqvist answered, "Not everything, no, but what He thinks I need to know in order to minister to my congregation. Sometimes He answers my questions in one manner or another."

Bjorn's face screwed up into a worried expression, and finally he said in a whisper loud enough for Caspar to hear, "Just don't ask Him how Lena got that bite mark on her arm, please. My mama thinks she did it to herself, and I want her to keep thinking that."

Pastor Lundqvist looked solemn and said, "Does someone else feel guilty for giving her that mark? I would tell that person that the only way to find peace is to confess and ask forgiveness before the Lord—and their mama."

Bjorn looked stubborn and said nothing, focusing on putting his feet in relatively dry parts of the street as they drew up in front of the shop. Behind him, Caspar was doing his best not to burst into open laughter, and Karin was holding Lena close, a disapproving scowl on her face.

Caspar stepped forward to open the door, and motioned the rest in before following and pulling it closed behind him.

Karin carried Lena up the stairs and called out behind herself, perhaps a bit frostily, "Bjorn, come up and get out of your good clothes. Then you and Lena will take your naps. On your own pallets, not together today," she added, and Caspar ducked his face out of Bjorn's view to hide his smile.

Then he saw Pastor Lundqvist's serious expression return,

and said hastily, "Let me just get some wood on this fire, and then you and I may talk."

He attended to the chore, trying to hide his nervousness in the mundane task, and then turned back to the pastor. Offering the other man the stool, Caspar sat on the edge of his sewing table and asked, "How can I be of service, Pastor Lundqvist?"

The pastor sat down and said, "A woman in my congregation came to me this week and confessed to me that she had taken an action for which she wanted to be absolved, as she had concluded that it might be sinful."

Caspar frowned. "I presume that happens often enough in your position, but I do not see how it is any of my business to hear about it."

"She said that she had acted against you, in particular, and had caused others to do so as well."

Understanding blossomed in Caspar's mind, and he nodded. "Ah, yes. While I do not know who started it, I had noted the fact that several customers had come to me and withdrawn business. I have commented about it to Karin, and while it is not a fatal blow to my shop, it is also not an insignificant one."

The pastor nodded. "That was my first concern when this woman confessed her misdeeds to me. As you may have perceived from my sermon today, I have become concerned about the tendency of people to blame others for their misfortunes. In particular, as our trade continues to be disrupted by our break from England, even with the peace, there is no longer the war to blame for their misfortunes, so people will look for new scapegoats."

Caspar nodded, wincing slightly. "And I can imagine that Mister Graff's accusations against me have helped to make me a natural target to attach blame to."

"Exactly," the pastor agreed. "I do not think that my sermon today was clear enough to change anybody's mind, but we must act as one nation now, else we will prove the worst of the naysayers in the English Parliament right, that we on this continent are too unsophisticated to run our own affairs."

He grimaced, and Caspar felt a burst of sympathy for the man. It must be difficult enough to have the responsibility for the souls of his congregation, without the added weight of trying to help in some small way as a new nation tried to find its footing. Lost in his own thoughts, he almost missed the pastor's next comment.

"And now I have heard a rumor that some of the most outspoken patriots are suggesting that they ought to find excuses to bring you additional work, which seems almost as dangerous to me as those who are taking work away based on your supposed sympathies."

Startled, Caspar replied, "Why, yes, I have seen some commissions for bespoke work apparently motivated as you describe, but I regarded that as providing a welcome counter to the lost business. And now you say that these jobs are a bad thing, too?"

The pastor shook his head in exasperation. "We cannot continue to have Patriot shops and Loyalist shops. We must have only American shops, or we will fracture back into conflict and war." He gave Caspar a pointed look. "And war is never good for businesses, no matter how welcome a particular job may be in the moment."

Chapter 16

Caspar was letting himself become lost in the smooth movement of his pencil over paper as he drew up the pattern for another gown, this one ordered by the wife of a former Continental Army officer from the town. She was apologetic for only having continental dollars with which to pay, but he had assured her that most people paid in continentals or in Delaware paper, and that he could conduct business in either.

He tried to keep his mind on his work, but his mind kept drifting back to the conversation with the pastor, and to the offhand comment that the man had made about the state of trade after the peace. He hadn't been paying close attention before he'd spoken to Pastor Lundqvist, but now, he had noticed that those who had taken business away from him were showing up in new clothes imported from England.

Such luxury goods had formerly either been smuggled—and correspondingly more expensive than locally made clothing—or hopelessly out of fashion, hoarded from before the war had begun. But some general questions to his preferred factors in the shipping trades had given him some answers.

Nearly immediately on the heels of the first ship bringing news of the terms of the peace treaty, English trading ships had been welcomed into the harbors of Philadelphia, Boston, New-York, and Charles-Town, carrying a wide variety of goods, including gowns made "in the latest style and of the highest quality materials," according to the handbill one factor had showed him.

While no gown made on the far side of the ocean from the woman who would wear it would ever be as fine as a bespoke one that he made from that same woman's measurements, these imported goods could undermine his business. Of course, on the other side of the coin, he could now get cloth from the markets in London, as well as from those in Paris or even India.

His factors were generally optimistic, although they pointed out that nearly all of this trade was on English ships, as very little American merchant shipping had survived the war. It would take years to rebuild the American merchant fleet, and until then, they would be at the mercy of whatever the English traders wanted to charge for shipping.

The factor he'd spoken to a few days past, after his conversation with the pastor, had said something else that had given Caspar pause. "Now, think of these circumstances you are aware of, and multiply them many fold. Nearly every market you can think of will be affected similarly. Things made here in America will be dear, while those coming from England will be expensive, but less expensive than local manufacture. Add tariffs between the states, and our domestic goods will be utterly unable to compete with those from England."

He'd grimaced. "Do not depend upon your customers having money to spend in the months ahead, my friend. A very few lucky ones may—at first. But sooner or later, we will all feel the pinch of the peace."

As much as the larger situation concerned him, though, Caspar had an immediate, urgent need to ensure that he could keep his shop open and continue to feed his family.

Karin's father had mentioned that his own finances were none too stable, so if they ran into trouble, there would be no relief from that direction. So long as he was willing and able to continue accepting Continental currency, there was some business from soldiers, many of whom had returned in the past two and a half years. Their enlistments were finished, and the war gave every sign of being over, so home they came, their purses full of devalued currency.

Soon enough, though, there would be no place left to spend the much-derided money, and more importantly, there would be none left to spend, anyway. Farmers in the districts around town were still planting crops, but with no assurance that they would find buyers. The same went for distillers, weavers, and shepherds. All had to proceed on faith in the future, knowing that they could not do very much to control the conditions in which their work would come to fruition.

At least, Caspar thought, looking around his cozy little shop, he did not have to start his work six months or more before any hope of seeing a profit from it. Yes, he had stocks of cloth on hand, but he had stopped stockpiling it against the anticipation of higher prices in the future.

Watching prices actually fall, his earlier strategy had seemed foolhardy, but it was based on his experience during wartime, and that was no guide to the markets of the peace. He sighed and scribed another smooth, soothing line onto the paper, the finished gown already taking shape in his mind.

A moving shadow from outside his window caused him to glance up, and he grimaced to see Mister van Dusen approaching his door. Sitting up and kneading the tension out of his lower back, Caspar faced the door as the other man gave the door a peremptory rap and immediately entered, not waiting to be acknowledged or invited inside.

For his part, Caspar did not feign politeness, as he asked, "Mister van Dusen, what brings you to my establishment? I had thought that we had parted under an understanding that we would not see things the same way in this lifetime."

Van Dusen favored him with a frown. "I come, *neighbor*"—he placed special stress on the word—"to advise you of a development that affects us both, and which I thought prudent to make you aware of as quickly as possible."

Caspar could not help but think that whatever Mister van Dusen had come to tell him, it could not possibly be good news. "What is that, *neighbor?*" Two could play at the game of words stressed without explanation.

"Mister Phillips, your landlord, has just passed into the next world this very afternoon, and it seems likely that his son will sell his holdings here in town and depart at his earliest opportunity to be with a girl he met while on business for his father in Philadelphia."

Caspar froze. If this news were true, it could upend everything that had seemed stable and reliable in his life in a matter of weeks. Mechanically, he said, "I am grieved to hear it. Mister Phillips has been a kind and conscientious landlord, and was a good man."

Mister van Dusen nodded in curt acknowledgment of Caspar's rote comments. With a malicious little smile, he said, "There are few in a position to purchase the old man's property from his son, but I thought it a kindness to inform you that the possibility exists that you could buy out your lease entirely. I am certain that the younger Mister Phillips would be happy to avoid disrupting your business."

Caspar said nothing, but they both knew that such a proposal was preposterous. The terms of the lease had been generous enough, but he had no repository of savings that would permit him to consider making an investment of that nature.

"Otherwise," van Dusen continued, his smile growing, "There are a few others who might consider this property to be a worthwhile investment. Why, I might even join with a few of my particular friends to pool our resources and see about buying this old place."

Now, the other man's smile had nearly reached his eyes, and he added, as though in an afterthought, "Of course, were we to do so, we would need to realize a profit from the venture, and that would doubtless mean increasing the rent to something more like what the market will support, instead of the bargain that I understand your father-in-law secured for you from Mister Phillips."

Wrinkling his nose in a show of distaste for the little shop, he said, "Perhaps we could get something of greater value in this space—for the good of the community, naturally. In any event, that was all the news of the day that I came to share. I can see that you have your work . . . cut out for you."

Chuckling at his sophomoric witticism, Mister van Dusen swept back out of the shop with as little regard for polite conduct as when he had entered.

Once he was certain that the man had truly departed, Caspar sat back on his feet atop the sewing table and permitted himself a moment to just shake in reaction to the news, and to van Dusen's thinly veiled threat.

He had long been aware that no sunrise was promised to any man, nor any certainty to any venture, but it still came as a shock to realize just how narrow a line laid between his present relative prosperity and utter ruin.

He took a deep breath then and reminded himself that it did no good to look at things in such absolute terms. Before they had gotten the shop, Caspar had conducted his business from a table in the corner of a public house; if it came to it, he could do the same again.

Mister Jacobson did not have a particularly spacious house, but in a desperate situation, Caspar, Karin, and the children could find a safe—if cramped—place to sleep at night. Karin's mother had even commented after church the prior week that she was sorry that they only all sat down to break bread together once a week, after church services.

And, of course, Caspar still needed to verify Mister van Dusen's poisonous suppositions, and exhaust all other avenues to resolve the difficulty that the man had gleefully laid out. Just because no obvious solution presented itself to his shocked and troubled mind did not mean that there was no solution possible.

It was clear that van Dusen had hoped to frighten Caspar into taking rash action, but the man had underestimated him. If he knew nothing else for certain now, Caspar knew that much.

Chapter 17

The funeral rites at their old landlord's church were different from those that Caspar was accustomed to, but they were not too strange to understand. The man's son, a spindly young man Caspar had only met once before, appeared before the other mourners, his eyes rimmed in red, and a well-used kerchief clutched in one hand.

"My-my father was proud to have lived to see the independence of our nation," he said, hesitantly, and in a voice that barely reached the back pews of the church, where Caspar sat. "He always told me that it was a day that had been fated to come about when the great Author of the world first made His plans for this continent."

He paused to blow his nose yet again, and then continued, "Although my father was too old to serve in any militia, and I was too young, we both found other ways to support the American cause." Unsure where the young man was going with this line of commentary, Caspar leaned forward in his pew, straining to make out his words.

"But this is not why you have gathered with me to remember my father. There will be other days on which to talk about his convictions and the charge that he laid upon me to carry out his wishes."

Caspar leaned back and let himself listen with half of his

attention on the young man's recollections of his childhood under the stern but loving eye of his father and his step-mother. The rest of his thoughts were pondering ways to approach this young man and attempt to negotiate terms under which he could keep the shop in its present space—and his family in their home.

He knew that it would be too soon to speak to Mister Phillips' son immediately after the funeral, but he did not want to wait so long as to permit van Dusen or others an opportunity to make a bid that would turn Caspar's life upside-down.

At least van Dusen was not at the funeral, circling like a vulture over a fresh corpse. Caspar grimaced to himself at the image, realizing that he was only sitting a short distance away from Mister Phillips' coffin as he imagined a scene with a carrion bird flying overhead.

Decency, though, might cost him everything, and was a luxury too dear to risk. He had consulted Mister Jacobson immediately, of course, and as he expected, that worthy man could offer nothing of greater value than advice.

The reverses of the past months seemed only to be speeding up, and few were in a position to invest in the well-being of a tailor and his family. Those who might have been in such a position were unwilling to help, and Caspar had quickly realized that his only hope lay in appealing to the son personally.

The younger Phillips' remembrances of his father having wound down with a final, prolonged honk into his handkerchief, the priest resumed his place at the pulpit and led the crowd through the prayers for the dead and an exhortation to carry on in Mister Phillips memory.

When the funeral was over, Caspar joined the line offering

Mister Phillips' son personal condolences. As he reached the young man, Caspar bowed respectfully, and said, "I sorrow for your loss, and I hope that your father's good works will find fresh expression in your life."

The younger Phillips nodded gravely and answered, "Indeed, that is all that I can hope for. His final wishes included some matters that touch upon your business with him, and I should like very much to discuss them with you at your earliest opportunity."

Caspar bowed again. "Your servant, sir. When should I call on you?"

The other man glanced at the line still snaking its way up the aisle of the little church. "Perhaps after the dinner hour this evening?"

"I will be honored to call on you then," Caspar said. "I do not wish to intrude upon your grief, but I am most eager to speak with you. Until then, sir."

He bowed one more time and stepped away to permit the next mourner to take his place. Walking back to his shop, he barely noticed that the weather was a substantial improvement over the past fortnight, clear and cold enough that the streets were now more frozen than muck. He was preoccupied with speculation over what Mister Phillips' final wishes might have been—and, more importantly, how the man's son intended to fulfill them.

He also took little note of the dinner that Karin had prepared, other than to be thankful that the last of the *vitergröt* was finally gone. He hadn't wanted to upset Karin by saying something, but the last couple of days from the big pot had definitely tasted a bit off to him. Nobody had gotten ill from it, though, so he supposed at the time that his palate was just more sensitive than the rest of the family's.

Tonight's meal was some sort of thick, savory soup, but if someone had asked him on the street afterward what color it had been, Caspar would not have been able to provide a certain answer. Karin had not pressed him for conversation, and the children had been uncharacteristically quiet and reserved at the sight of their father in his black mourning clothes.

Caspar had donned the outfit to show respect for the dead man, rather than out of any particular sorrow at his passing. The few times they had spoken, Phillips had struck him as an honest man, content to charge a fair rent, rather than gouging him for every possible sixpence. Another man might have justified to himself raising the rent sharply when soldiers started returning from the war, but Phillips had adhered to the initial agreement he'd struck with Karin's father.

Walking now toward the Phillips home, his woolen cloak pulled tightly around him, Caspar wondered whether there was any hope of the son continuing his father's benign management of the property, or whether van Dusen's most sinister threats were within the scope of reality.

With no conclusions, and not enough information to reach any, Caspar arrived at the door to Mister Phillips' home and rapped smartly, then waited to be answered.

Phillips' house slave, an enormous man with skin nearly as dark as his eyes, opened the door and greeted him. "Mister Schmidt, my master is expecting you. Follow me, sir."

Entering the study, Caspar was immediately aware that the younger Mister Phillips seemed to have been weeping again, as evidenced by the pale, watery look of his eyes and the redness of his nose. He sat in a comfortable chair to one side of a small table, a nearly full glass of wine at his hand.

Again, Caspar bowed and said, "Thank you for seeing me under these difficult circumstances."

The other man waved dismissively and said, "Please, sit, Mister Schmidt. My father would be appalled to see me carrying on so. In his last days, he told me, 'Death comes for us all, son, and I have had a better life than most. Do not weep for the end of a race I have run well.'"

Caspar nodded. "I can only hope to be so philosophical when my time comes, Mister Phillips."

"Please, call me Edward," the younger man said.

"Certainly, Edward, and I am Caspar." He offered his hand across the table, and they shook solemnly.

"Caspar, what I have to tell you may come as a surprise, but I hope it will not be an unwelcome one. Yesterday, I was visited by a man—I think his name was Vanderson or some such, and he treated me with rude disregard, telling me I had a financial obligation to sell him your shop, and that he would make me a handsome price for it."

Certain that it was van Dusen who had approached the man, Caspar had to remind himself to breathe as Phillips continued, "In truth, even if I had been a position where I was obliged to sell, I would not have wanted to strike a deal with him. He did not appear to be the sort of man who could afford a purchase like that without backing, and he refused to say who was helping him in his quest."

He made a sour face and said, "The man seemed to assume

that your history as a soldier in the service of the Crown, and his accusation that you had departed that service . . . irregularly, would sway me in his favor. He made the mistake of thinking that I must have harbored Loyalist sympathies, given my father's wealth."

He again made a dismissive gesture with his hand. "However, as I started to explain at his funeral before I thought better of the occasion, my father was a fervent patriot, and wanted his passing to further the cause of the independence he was so glad to have seen. In consequence of this, my father's final wishes were very clear."

Caspar knew his face must have revealed the confusion he was feeling, because the young man smiled gently and said, "I see that none of this is explaining to you what I must do with the property you occupy. My father instructed me to deed it to the government of the state, so that they might reduce their debts by whatever small value it carries."

Feeling as though he had been struck by a cannon ball, Caspar gasped aloud. "But what of my shop and my family? What is to become of us?"

"Well, my father wanted the value of the property to go to the government but this Vanderson fellow so annoyed me that when he let slip that he hoped to dispossess you by acquiring the place, I applied myself to the question of how to both thwart his purposes and meet my father's. I believe that I have arrived at a strategy to do both."

He took a deep breath and said, "I should like to offer you tenancy for as long as is convenient for you, on the same terms as you had with my father, except that your rent will be payable directly to the state."

Caspar could hardly believe his ears. Had van Dusen somehow so alienated this grief-stricken man that he had managed to undermine his entire fell purpose? It seemed so, and Caspar said a quick prayer to thank God for foolish enemies.

"Mister Phillips, I would be most grateful to accept your very kind offer. This Mister van Dusen had indeed made representations to me that you would need to sell the property you had inherited, and that he intended to use this to my disadvantage."

He took a long, shaky breath, and said, "Thank you for your wisdom, and for your wholly unexpected kindness."

Chapter 18

Cross-legged on his sewing table, Caspar knew he should get back to work putting the finishing touches on the gown, but he just couldn't seem to muster the concentration to do so. His mind kept turning over the incredible conversation with Edward Phillips, and its wholly unexpected outcome.

He felt light, as though a crushing weight he had never felt building up on his shoulders had been abruptly removed, leaving him in danger of floating right up to the ceiling.

He still hadn't formulated just how to share the news with Karin, never mind Mister Jacobson. He had mentioned van Dusen's threat to his wife, and she had only frowned and advised him to not borrow trouble from the future when there was ample to be found in the present. If nothing else, he owed her the courtesy of telling her that she had been correct about that.

Once the gown was finished, he had no new commissions lined up, and a trickle of just a few small repairs would not be enough to both feed the family and pay the rent on the shop. He took a deep breath and reached for the gown, arranging the cloth so that he could put in the long, loose stitches of the temporary hem. The more exacting final stitches would go in, of course, after the client came back in for the fitting.

He had gotten no further than halfway through the hem when the door flew open, banging against the wall behind it.

Thinking that he must have failed to latch it properly, letting the wind throw it open, Caspar scowled at himself and started to set the gown aside.

The Mister van Dusen stepped into the doorway, his eyes flashing with rage. The Dutchman spat, "So, you've talked the Phillips boy into practically giving you this shop, I understand? Some legal trickery with assigning the rents to the state, so that none will dare to interfere, am I right? Well, I will do what I must to stop you, just you wait!"

Caspar did not have to pretend to gawk at van Dusen. His mouth sagged open as he took in the man's appearance. Barely dressed for the weather, an old coat tied around his waist haphazardly, and his hat jammed onto a wigless head, the man looked frankly ridiculous, and his words only contributed to the effect of a person who had taken leave of their senses.

Finally, Caspar said mildly, "Do come in and close the door, that we may speak without letting the winter come to live in the house for good."

This seemed to enrage van Dusen even more, and he stood defiantly in the doorway, pulling his coat closer around himself. "You shall heat the outdoors all the way to Philadelphia, for all that I care, sir. In any event, I will not tarry any longer than it takes me to tell you that you will fail in this scheme that you have convinced Phillips' son to go along with. If I have to take it all the way to the Privy Council, I will do so. I am not without friends at the very top of our government, even now."

Caspar considered explaining that the plan had been Edward's own idea, but decided that to do so would only inflame the Dutchman further. Instead, he said only, "That is your right, of course, although I could caution you against making yourself too visibly an opponent of the independence and the peace. Both are fairly well thought of in Dover, I anticipate."

If his intent was to pacify the other man, it failed spectacularly, as van Dusen seemed to lose even the power of speech for a long moment, gesticulating and making strangled noises before he shouted, "The Tories have the Council, and after the election this fall, you may expect that they will also have the Assembly! After that, we shall see, my friend. We shall see. Your little trick will be overturned, and this property will return to the market, where it should have been as soon as Mister Phillips went to his reward."

Caspar found that he wasn't even intimidated by the man's bluster now. Knowing that young Phillips was managing the property in accordance with his father's wishes, and trusting that the young man would have sought advice on the matter before proceeding, he did not worry that the Council or the Assembly would act against the interests of the treasury and turn away the rent payments.

He supposed that any man could be tempted by the opportunity for an outright sale, but the uncertainty of that in the current climate of fear and disruption did not lie as heavily on the balance as did the relative certainty of a steady rental payment. If it were his property, he would surely keep the tenants on, at least until the market settled down.

Van Dusen appeared to be waiting for some response from him, so Caspar said, "We shall see, then, sir, in due time. Meanwhile, could I trouble you to close the door as you leave?"

It was about as direct as he could be without an open

breach of polite decorum, and for a moment, Caspar wondered if the man might suffer a stroke of apoplexy on the spot. He observed dispassionately as a vein on van Dusen's forehead visibly swelled and pulsed for a moment, before the man shook his head and slammed the door shut, knocking a wooden box of pins from the shelf beside his counter to the floor with the impact.

Caspar frowned, making a mental note to store them in a more secure location, as he climbed down from the table. As he stepped down, he felt a sharp pain in his toe, and stooped, annoyed, to pull a pin out of the bottom of the digit. As he had needed to explain to Karin on more than one occasion, it made no sense to wear shoes up onto the sewing table, but it was moments such as this that made him question the wisdom of his habits. The wound did not bleed, so he dismissed it from his mind and went about gathering up the rest of the sharp tools of his trade, so that the children would not hurt themselves.

The impact had bent the hinges on the box, and he fussed with those until he could re-close it, latching the lid securely to prevent another spill. He placed the box on the shelves closer to his sewing table, which was where it should have been to begin with. He'd taken it down when he was working on assembling the panels of the gown, and hadn't yet put it away properly. His toe throbbed to emphasize that he should have been more careful.

Sighing, he realized that van Dusen had cost him the very last of the light of the day, so he went back to the table to fold up the gown and put it away, to be finished the next day. He pinched out the tapers and barred the door to finish closing up his shop for the night.

Climbing upstairs, he thought again about what to tell

Karin about Edward's extraordinary offer, and the promise of stability that it gave them. There was no need to report van Dusen's nonsense—although she may have already heard it from upstairs, it was of so little import that it did not merit worrying her about.

Emerging into the kitchen, he found her sitting on her chair next to the table, cradling a sleeping Lena, a gentle smile on her face. She put a finger on her lips and nodded toward the children's sleeping pallet, where Bjorn lay curled up, his thumb in his mouth as he slept.

Caspar could not imagine how both children had slept through the commotion of van Dusen's visit, but he was glad to see that they were both at rest. He brushed a kiss across the top of his wife's head and sat in his own chair. The discussion he wanted to have with her could wait.

He closed his eyes and let his head down onto his arms atop the table. Despite having only walked to the church and then the Phillips home, he felt wearier than he had since that long ago day when he had fled from the battlefield.

A body could only take so much anticipation in any one day, he decided, and he had endured more in the time since he'd awakened that morning than he could recall having experienced in any one week previously. It all took a toll, and he was ready for an early supper and bedtime.

He heard Lena start to fuss and opened his eyes to see Karin attending to her. She said, quietly, "Could you check the stew to see whether it is done? The meat was from an old ox and was still tough the last time I checked it."

He smiled and rose from the table. "Of course, my dear," he said. "I am grateful that you could find meat that we could afford at all. If it is a bit toothsome, that is no great barrier to a well-prepared appetite."

She shook her head in mock disapproval of his accommodating attitude and turned back to taking care of Lena. Fishing a small piece of meat out of the broth, Caspar blew on it to cool it enough to avoid blistering his mouth, and then sampled it.

Nodding his approval, he said, "I can tell that this was an experienced beast, but he eats well enough now. Have the children already been fed?"

"Bjorn had just some broth, and was too tired to stay awake any longer. I expect that he'll be up before the cock crows tomorrow. Lena will nurse again before we retire, but she won't need any of the stew. It is just the two of us for supper tonight."

"Very good," he said, a genuine smile on his face. "We have a lot to discuss."

Chapter 19

The new owner of the gown had pronounced herself delighted with the work. Two of the customers who had withdrawn commissions had come back to reinstate them quietly since he'd delivered the gown, so Caspar had enough to keep him occupied, and more importantly, enough work to keep up with his obligations.

The toe he'd stuck with a pin had swollen up, and it throbbed as he worked on drawing out the pattern for a pair of breeches. Fortunately, he had made so many of this particular item over the years that he could almost do the work in his sleep.

Karin had applied poultices and, when snow had fallen again, had made him put his whole foot in a bucket she had filled from a clean spot behind the shop. She had relented only when he had complained that he could no longer feel any of his toes at all, but even this radical treatment had not helped, as the pain returned in full force once his foot regained feeling.

Caspar sighed, and when his toe gave a particularly nasty throb, he resolved to see the only man in town whose physic he trusted, just as soon as he finished sketching out the pattern.

It wasn't the first time he'd stuck himself on a pin or needle, and he knew it was unlikely to be the last, but there was something particularly galling about it coming this time because of van Dusen's little display of pique.

As for that poisonous little man, Caspar had heard nothing further of his intended interference with Edward Phillips' plans. He had been fairly confident that nothing would come of it, but the more time that passed, the better he felt about relying on being able to maintain the shop and their home without resorting to desperate measures.

After drawing out the last lines of the initial pattern, Caspar got down from the sewing table and made his way to the door for his boots and cape. Jamming a knitted woolen cap over his ears, he called upstairs, "Karin, I am going out to have Mister Canter look at my toe."

As though it could recognize that he was talking about it, the toe in question offered another powerful pulse of pain, this time echoed by a throb in his head. Karin called back, "Mind that you tell him what I have already done, so that he does not try to physic you in the same manner."

"Yes, my dear, I will tell him what treatments you have performed." With that, he made his way outside and started through the streets to the man's house.

The town was prettier now, with an even coating of snow softening and concealing all of its rough edges. The streets were a notable exception, the ruts from passing wagons marking ugly brown lines along the middle of the street, with a churned-up morass between, where the horse's hooves had passed through.

At least the edges of the streets were relatively clean, packed snow and ice. If it was more treacherous footing, at least a man did not risk ruining his clothes as he walked there. Turning onto the main street of the town, Caspar's headache returned with a fresh throb, and he clenched his jaw in concentration on the job of navigating to the medical man's house.

Knocking at the man's door, he heard a gruff voice summon him in. "It's unlocked, so enter quickly and keep the cold humors without."

Slipping through the door and closing it firmly behind himself, Caspar said through gritted teeth, "Mister Canter, I have suffered an injury in my shop that has exceeded my wife's power to cure. I hope that you have at your disposal some more effective means than we have in our home."

Canter motioned to the chair facing him, beside the fire. "Hang your cloak and take off your boots, then come and sit, and tell me about your injury."

Caspar described how he'd hurt himself and what Karin had done to help. Canter nodded, saying, "Very smart, using ice to quench the choleric humour with cool and wet. Your wife has excellent instincts. Let me have a look at the injury."

Caspar pulled off his stocking and rested his foot on Mister Canter's knee as the man indicated. The doctor felt along the length of Caspar's foot, from the heel forward, and elicited a yelp of pain from him when he squeezed the swollen toe between his fingers and thumb.

The man pursed his lips and looked up at Caspar. "I believe I may need to lance this toe, my friend, though we can likely avoid bleeding you. It is the choleric, not the sanguine humour that has become out of balance."

He looked up at Caspar, who was still wincing from the pressure of the doctor's fingers around his toe. "Perhaps first you should like a few drops of laudanum to dull the pain. I will not deceive you; this is likely to hurt more than most anything you have experienced in quite some time."

Caspar grimaced, and said through clenched teeth, "Then, by all means, you must administer the laudanum before you begin."

The doctor turned and pulled a small bottle from the shelf behind him, and measured out a dose. "Drink this straight away, and never think to stop and try the flavor of it. There is nothing to it that can recommend it on that account, but I assure you it will both give you relief from the pain that has brought you here, and render you insensate of the operation I must perform upon you."

Caspar did as he was told, though it seemed as though his mouth were strangely aware of the bitter draught he sought to pour into it. It was with an effort of will that he forced the glass past his lips, and, as promised, the medicine was bitter and unpleasant to the taste. Wrinkling his face, Caspar coughed and gasped as he handed the glass back to the doctor.

"Come and lie upon the table here, and I will secure you to it so that I may operate without concern that you might move about and cause yourself further injury upon my instruments."

Caspar felt somewhat hesitant, but the necessity persuaded him, and he laid down as instructed. Drawing leather straps about his torso, ankles, and wrists, as well as one to secure his head, the doctor pronounced himself satisfied and turned to the hearth.

"I will use a cauterizing blade, which will minimize the bloodletting as I operate. Once it is heated, I will begin."

Caspar said nothing, but merely tried to relax himself while he waited. Already, it seemed to him, the pain in his toe was lessened, and his head no longer seemed to ache, either. If nothing else, those improvements were already worth the trouble to come here. He felt a rising sense of confusion, and wondered where Karin was, as he was starting to feel very drowsy . . .

Some time later, he awoke, finding a strap across his chest holding him to the table where he lay. He called out groggily, "*Wa-warum bin ich hier fest-festgebunden?*" Remembering himself, he repeated, this time in English, "Why am I tied?"

The doctor came into view, smiling broadly. "You are secured to the table only to keep you from rolling off. The operation was a complete success, and the excess choleric humor drained quite satisfactorily in the course of it."

He waved a hand at Caspar's foot, now wrapped in cloth bandages. "I will accompany you back to your shop, as you should not venture forth without someone to ensure that you find your way in safety. In addition, you should not step onto that foot for a few days."

Still trying to clear his head, Caspar said, with difficulty, "That will make it hard for me to climb into my home above the shop."

"Aye, that cannot be avoided, then, but you should step so that you do not strain the wound where I had to release the choler. Let us get you home, though, before the laudanum wears off completely and you regain full sensation in that foot." He reached across Caspar and undid the buckle to the strap that secured him.

Helping Caspar into one boot and draping his cloak around his shoulders, the doctor positioned himself under his arm on the side with the wound and said, "Shall we, then?"

The hobble home was awkward, and all the more so for needing to keep his bandaged foot completely off the ground. Fortunately, Mister Canter had experience at helping others similarly limited, and they made their way to the door of the shop in decent time.

Caspar was happy to get there, as the promised return of sensation was coming upon him with greater speed and intensity than he expected, based on what the doctor had told him. Worse, his headache had returned, as well, and he could not seem to keep from clenching his teeth in reaction.

Entering the shop, he turned and said, as clearly as he could manage, "Thank you, sir, for your physicking, and for the help getting home. What will your fee be for these services?"

The man scoffed, and said, "It was all in a day's work. The laudanum is dear stuff, even with the war over, though. Has to be brought in from China, don't you know? But nothing else answers the way it does for the sort of situation you presented."

Caspar nodded, impatient to make his way upstairs and take to his bed.

Sensing his eagerness, the doctor said, "All together, I think that eight shillings should cover it."

Caspar hopped on one foot over to his counter and opened the hasp on his money box. He handed over the notes to the doctor, saying through still-gritted teeth, "I thank you again for your assistance."

The doctor gave him a puzzled look and asked, "Are you in so much pain so soon that you must clench your mouth like that?"

Caspar replied, "My foot does pain me, but my jaw seems to have a mind of its own in this matter."

The doctor frowned deeply and asked, "Does your head ache, as well, my friend, or does your neck feel tight?"

Caspar nodded, saying, "Head hurts, yes."

Mister Canter took a deep breath and blew it out gustily.

"We must get you into bed immediately, and I will go back to my abode for some additional physic to treat you properly. I fear, Mister Schmidt, that you may be developing lockjaw."

Chapter 20

L ying in his bed, his face drawn back into an involuntary rictus of a maniacal grin, Caspar drew one slow, deliberate breath after another. He could feel the muscles of his back pulling tight, and the doctor had warned him that before the disease ran its course, he might struggle to breathe.

That feared development had not arrived, but the seemingly never-ending panic he felt at losing control of his body left him needing to focus on keeping his breathing deep and even. The doctor had assured him that with proper dosing and care, most of those he had seen afflicted with lockjaw recovered themselves in a matter of weeks.

But in a conversation with Karin by the hearth that Caspar could overhear, the doctor had said that those weeks would be exhausting for the patient and his carers alike. He had advised Karin to seek help from friends, family, and neighbors for the trial that lay before them.

Many times, Caspar had heard one voice or another in conversation with Karin, downstairs, but he could not identify many of them, nor very often make out what was being said. He could only be sure of Karin's parents, and a couple of people from the church congregation. Pastor Lundqvist, of course, had come and prayed with Caspar, but he was glad enough that the man had not brought out the anointing oil of the last rites.

Caspar had no clear sense of how many days he had passed, confined to his bed, listening to the children play and Karin perform her many household duties. In the mornings and evenings, she sat alongside their bed and patiently spooned plain broth into his mouth. He had found that swallowing had become difficult, so she had learned to wait until he had gotten his throat to cooperate before offering him more.

She had to attend to all of his needs, even those that were the most humiliating to Caspar, on top of taking care of the children, and he found himself questioning what he could ever have done in his life to deserve such devotion from her.

This was, of course, only one of the many thoughts that raced through his mind during his waking hours. Though his body refused his commands, he was perfectly aware of his surroundings, and as she washed his face, Karin often discovered streaks down his cheeks where his tears had left their traces.

Caspar was grateful for Mister Canter's visits, particularly as the doctor often dosed him not only with a range of physic that he assured Karin were specifics for the symptoms of lockjaw, but also, if Caspar appeared to be in particular distress, a few drops of the blessed laudanum.

Ordinary sleep was only a partial relief from the terrors of the dread disorder, but the medicine permitted him to sink into a slumber that was actually restful, at least for a few hours.

Then came the day when Caspar realized that his back had relaxed perceptibly from its terrible spasms of the prior afternoon. When Karin came to bring him his morning broth, he managed to grunt something that sounded a bit like "Thank you." And when Lena's shriek rent the air, as Bjorn stole a toy from her, or some other provocation, he did not groan in agony as he had for days on end at any sound that disturbed his slumber.

The following day, he could even swallow without difficulty, and with each passing day, his condition improved further. Mister Canter pronounced himself fully satisfied with Caspar's recovery and predicted that he would be up and out of bed within a fortnight.

While he was grateful to be on the mend, Caspar was anxious about the state of their affairs. He had thought of little else but the new rental agreement Edward Phillips had delivered just before the beginning of his ordeal. As soon as he had recovered the power of speech, Caspar croaked to Karin, "How much money left?"

Karin smiled and put another spoonful of broth in his mouth, shaking her head. "We will speak of it when you are more fully recovered, my dear," she said.

Caspar swallowed impatiently, and asked urgently, "But the rent?" Even he was surprised at how hoarse and raspy his voice sounded.

Karin pursed her mouth and spooned up another mouthful of broth. She said, "There is nothing for you to worry about, Caspar, except eating and regaining your strength."

Caspar's brows knitted in a weak scowl—his face was still not fully his own to command—but he opened his mouth for the spoon.

After he'd finished his dinner, he tried once more as she stood to leave. "Will we lose shop?"

Karin sighed and said, "No, my dear, the matter is taken care of. Since you will not let it wait, I will tell you of it now."

She sat back down and said, "One of our first visitors when

news spread that you had fallen ill was Mister Phillips. He was also concerned about the matter of our rent, and came to find out whether we would be able to pay it in a timely fashion without you being able to work."

Caspar frowned, feeling as though his concerns were being proved valid despite her assurances, but she continued, "When I told him I did not believe that we had sufficient savings to maintain our rent during your convalescence, he instantly laid the amount needed for three months' time on the counter, and would hear nothing from me about terms for repayment."

Her eyes welled up in recalled gratitude. "Caspar, he was only the first of many of our friends who came and offered whatever we might need to get through this. Your customers came with gifts of food and words of encouragement. My childhood friends made sure that the children wanted for nothing."

Her eyes wide with wonder, she said, "Even some of those who have lately set themselves up as our detractors, based on some dedication to old resentments, have come around with kind things to say."

Caspar realized that he, too, was in danger of crying, and he quipped hoarsely, "van Dusen or Graff?"

Karin smiled despite herself. "No, neither of them made an appearance. I don't suppose that either of them wishes you dead, but neither are they likely to be unhappy at any misfortune that befalls you."

Then she gave him an uncertain frown, and added, "Still, had they intended to take advantage of your illness, I would have expected to have heard something of it from some of the people who did come to visit."

Her expression cleared, and she patted him on the shoulder. "Rest, my dear, and be secure in the knowledge that all will be well. Your only responsibility at this time is to eat and grow stronger. Mister Canter will be by this evening to see how you are doing, and I know he will be pleased to see you so improved."

She left, and Caspar could hear her feeding the children something for dinner—he realized that for the first time since he'd fallen ill, whatever she'd prepared for dinner made his mouth water, and he wondered how much longer it might be before the doctor would tell her he could again eat real food.

But the primary focus of his thoughts was his amazement at the generosity of their friends and neighbors. Mister Phillips' loan— or gift?—warmed his heart, but he had known that the young man had already skirted his own father's wishes to help Caspar keep his shop and home. Seeing Karin overcome at the memory of the other kindnesses they had received, though, made him eager for the details.

As a newcomer to the community, he had been aware of the ties of long association and even blood that bound it together, but he had never felt himself to be a party to those ties. Seeing it manifested in a kind comment or a knowing look between others had always left him feeling somewhat wistful for that sense of belonging and of being valued.

Had it taken an illness that had threatened his life to make him aware that he was, in fact, a part of that community, that he belonged, that he was valued on his own terms, and not just as the husband from away of someone who had grown up among them?

The question—and its apparent answer—nagged at him, and he wondered whether he might have gone to his grave unaware that his clients thought of him as more than merely a useful means of getting the clothing they needed, but saw him as a man whose family depended upon him, whose value to the community went beyond his skill as a tailor. In a strange way, the crisis that still left him confined to his sickbed might be the most wonderful thing that had ever happened to him. He drifted off to sleep pondering this realization, and feeling at peace for the first time in months.

Chapter 21

Today was, at long last, the day when Mister Canter had given Caspar leave to venture down the steep stairs back to his shop. He had been rising from his bed and moving about his home for nearly a fortnight, and although he still felt unsteady on his feet after a frustratingly short time, he was eager to reacquaint himself with the world beyond the few small rooms he shared with his family.

When he'd first gotten up from his bed and had taken a few shuffling steps, supported on one side by Karin and on the other by Mister Canter, Bjorn had watched, wide-eyed, from his pallet. Karin had banished the children to the confines of their beds, lest they get underfoot during the process of Caspar trying his legs again.

Solemnly, Bjorn said, "Lena walks better than you do, Papa."

Caspar smiled grimly at his son. "Indeed she does, Bjorn. But we're going to try to get me to the point where I can even outrun you again, all right?"

At that point, Caspar's legs started to shake, and he motioned with his chin that Karin and the doctor should return him to the bed. Bjorn looked skeptical and said, "Papa, if you ever want to catch me, you will need to try harder than that."

Caspar sat down heavily on the bed and said, "I will, son.

I will."

And today, he was pushing himself harder, standing unaided and walking over to the stairs. His stride was still not as unconsciously confident as it had been before the illness, but neither was he shuffling about or unsteady on his feet.

The children asleep for their naps, Karin had gone down to the shop before him, and stood at the bottom of the stairs, looking up anxiously at him. He wasn't sure what she meant to do if he lost his footing. Although he was a mere shadow of his former self, he was still too large a man for her to catch. Yet there she stood, ready to try. Once again, he wondered just how he had come to deserve such devotion.

Instead of going down the stairs facing forward as usual, he turned around and felt his way down with one foot and then the other, holding on to the wall and then the top stairs as he reached the bottom. Stepping off the last stair and turning, he said, "There, you see? Not too difficult at all. Now, let us see how the shop looks."

Gazing through the front window for the first time in weeks, he was unsurprised to see that the blanket of clean snow was gone, revealing the muddy street and solid gray skies outside. Too early for the trees to have unfolded their leaves, they stood as stark, skeletal forms. It was the most beautiful scene Caspar could ever remember having beheld.

He walked over to the counter, aware of Karin's eyes following him, and he leaned against it for support, but smiled broadly at her. "It is good to be out of that bed," he said. "I do not believe that I will try to work today—I do not think that my hands are steady enough yet to take up the cutting and stitching—

but perhaps we can have a fire in the hearth down here and just sit for a while?"

She nodded and stooped to lay the fire. Caspar walked over and put his hand on her shoulder. "Let me, my dear."

"Are you sure? I know you are impatient to recover your former strength, but I do not want you to try so hard that you do yourself more injury."

He sighed gustily. "Yes, Karin, I am sure that I can manage this chore. You deserve a rest, after all that you have had to do. Go, sit." He crouched beside her and gently took the kindling from her.

Although she looked ready to say something in reply, she instead shook her head, her lips pressed into a disapproving line, and did as he bade her. Turning back to the hearth, Caspar smiled to himself at the minor victory, and did a careful job of arranging the wood and added the char cloth he retrieved from the tinderbox next to the hearth.

Striking a long spark into the tinder with a practiced hand, he blew upon the tiny ember it lit until it leaped into flame. He gave it a moment to gain some momentum and then blew again until some of the kindling had caught. Satisfied, he put away the flint and steel into the tinderbox and stood to make his way to the stool opposite Karin. He did not reveal the wave of dizziness that came over him as he stood, but he was grateful to sit.

Taking her hand into his own, he said, "I know well that my illness has been at least as hard for you as it was for me. You kept the household in order, spoke with my customers on my behalf, and cared for me when I was as helpless as an infant. I have not the words—I do not think that the words exist—to describe the depth of my gratitude to you."

Her previous expression of irritation dissolved completely, and she blushed under his praise. "I did only what had to be done, my husband. Had our positions been reversed, you would have done no less for me."

He scoffed. "I would have tried, but I would have utterly failed. I know nothing of the arts you practice as your daily routine. The children would have gone unfed, unclothed, and undisciplined. You are far more capable than I am."

She gave him a reproachful look. "Do not give yourself so little credit, Caspar. You would at least have kept them clothed." A sly smile played over her lips, and she looked at him fondly.

He burst out laughing and shook his head. "Do you see? You outdo me even in the matter of offering compliments. Very well, I suppose that I might have been competent to keep clothing on them, but without food or guidance, that would have been of little use."

Then his expression sobered, and he said, "In all solemnity, though, I should like to hear more about those who helped us in this time of our need. As much as I know you did, I also know that they helped you, and I would like the opportunity to repay their kindness when they come to their need."

She replied, "Truly, I did not keep an accounting. So many people dropped off dinners that I actually had to cook only occasionally. Others came to add to your order-book, so that once you are recovered, you likely have work to last through the summer. Some of those insisted on making deposits, even though I warned them that Mister Canter was uncertain of your recovery."

Caspar's eyebrows rose at this. "He never spoke to me of this possibility."

"No, but he told me that the speed of your illness's onset reminded him of a case where he could not save the patient, and that I must prepare myself for the possibility of the worst happening."

Caspar looked at her with fresh respect. "In that case, you kept your wits about you and do all that needed to be done, even as you were contemplating your widowhood? I gave you too little praise, my wife."

She acknowledged his compliments with a smile, though her eyes had welled up with unshed tears. "The worst times were when I came to care for you and saw that you had been weeping, though you could not speak. I knew then that you were suffering in your mind, and not just in your body."

His gaze turned to the fire, which was warming up the shop nicely. His eyes seemed to contemplate something at a great distance, and he said nothing for a long moment. Finally, he nodded. "I remember many times when I was awake and aware of my struggle, though I do not remember weeping. I will be happy if I never need to think of those days again, however."

Wiping his own eyes as he saw her do likewise, he stared into the fire for a moment longer to collect himself again.

Turning back to look at her, he said, "I should rather think about the days that lie ahead than the ones I have just escaped. Work to last me through the summer, you say? Who recorded the orders?"

He had always kept his order-book in German, as he was most comfortable with the terminology and notations that he'd learned during his apprenticeship, and he found that as welcome as the business was, he was unaccountably defensive at the thought of someone else having made entries in their own manner.

Karin shrugged. "I still can't read very much even in English, and I could make no sense at all of what you'd written, so I asked each of the customers to write down in their own words what they wanted of you, and if they left a deposit, I asked them to write that in, as well."

Caspar had to see for himself what the result looked like, so he rose without a word and went to the counter. Flipping the book open, he turned to the last page he'd written on, and started reading through the entries that followed.

"For J. van Wert, 1 overdress, pockets; deposit 2 pounds. To L. Kaden, 2 pairs breeches, 1 each in blue and green, 3 pounds deposit. For H. Karlson, 1 shift in linen, no deposit." Entry after entry, for more than three full pages in various hands, the orders went on, and the deposits that were recorded were often far more than the finished items would even cost.

He looked up at Karin in wonder. "I believe that you have understated how much work our friends have given me. I shall be all the summer and into autumn completing all of this."

Karin smiled, her eyes bright again. "There will be more, too, when people hear you are recovered. Some did not know how to record what they wanted of you, and a few admitted they had no letters either."

Caspar shook his head, a puzzled look on his face. "What have I ever done to deserve such good fortune? I am an ordinary man, and although I like to think that I offer a good value in the work I give people, I have changed nobody's life by my presence here. Why are people choosing to be so kind to me?"

She smiled again, saying, "You truly do not understand? You are a good man, and that is more than many can manage in this world. You do not take short-cuts in your work, and you are honest about your mistakes and flaws."

He started to object, but she raised a hand to silence him. "Even when people set themselves up in opposition to you for your imagined past, you do not permit yourself to wallow in rage or self-pity, but bear their accusations in silence and permit your actions to speak on your behalf."

He gave her a half-smile and said, "If you hadn't stopped me, I believe that I would have struck Willem and bound myself to an affair of honor with him, so I am not as fine and perfect a human being as you would have me be."

"And yet, you let my words stop your hand. You are a good man, and one who deserves the care and goodwill that has flowed your way during this ordeal."

He bowed his head for a moment, then looked up at her and said, "Thank you. I shall endeavor to be worthy of it all."

Chapter 22

Entering church the following Sunday for the first time in months was both strange and wonderful. The familiar pews beckoned to him, and friends and neighbors greeted him with genuine joy at his recovery. Sitting down with Mister Jacobson on one side, and Karin on the other felt like another homecoming. His strength had not yet completely returned, but he had managed the walk to the church unassisted.

Even those who had revealed themselves to have had Tory leanings, canceling orders and shunning him, seemed happy to see him restored to his place with his family.

The service was familiar and comfortable, despite the differences from what he had grown up with. Rising and singing felt like an act of true thanks to the Lord, and to the men and women surrounding him on Earth.

Pastor Lundqvist's sermon was on healing the brokenness of the world, and the example the Lord gave in the story of the sinful woman who interrupted a dinner to weep upon his feet and beg forgiveness. She was, the pastor reminded them, bidden to go in peace, and advised that her faith had saved her.

The pastor related the judgment of His dining companions against the woman to the judgment that men of the world might have against one another, and reminded the congregation that what mattered to the Lord was their faith in Him. Through that, he added gently, even the most sinful among them could be forgiven.

Caspar couldn't help but think that the pastor was speaking directly to those who had been holding grudges on one side or the other of the peace and reminding them that judgment was not ultimately in their hands.

Caspar pondered this message through the rote actions that followed the sermon, wondering whether he was guilty of judgment against his neighbors. But then, what was he to do against the reckless hatred of van Dusen and his resentments driven by childhood disappointments? How was he to answer the baseless accusations made against him by Sergeant Graff?

He knew the Bible advised one to turn the other cheek in such circumstances, but how was that possible when doing so would result in harm to not only himself, but his wife and children? He had found no satisfactory answers by the time that the service wound to its conclusion, and he wondered whether those who had acted against him would find any more resolution from the sermon.

At the door, the pastor greeted him warmly. "If is so very good to see you back among our number, Mister Schmidt. When I spoke with your physician, he was uncertain as to your recovery, but I told him I had no doubt about your inner strengths."

Caspar nodded appreciatively. "When you visited and did not administer the last rites, I felt certain that I had a chance of restoration."

The pastor's eyebrows lifted. "I would not have thought that you were conscious during that visit. You gave every appearance of a man in an impenetrable fight with the Devil himself."

"I don't know if it was the Devil," Caspar said with a smile. "Mister Canter seemed to think that it was a gross imbalance of my humours. Either way, I was awake and aware, though trapped inside of a body that was at the command of forces outside of myself. If this seems consistent with a battle against Old Nick, then I will not argue with you."

He shook his head, as though to shake loose the memories that gathered in his mind. "All I will say is that I am happy to no longer be in the grips of that fight, and back into the ordinary world of good neighbors and good friends."

"And we are happy to have you back. Go in peace, and may God's blessings be upon you." Caspar nodded deeply again in thanks and turned to leave, Karin and the children following behind him.

Outside the door, a stout, flinty-eyed man caught sight of him and hurried over. "Caspar Schmidt?"

"Yes, that is me," he confirmed.

"I am Magistrate Johnson, and there is a matter I must discuss with you urgently."

"Can I accompany my family home first, or does this matter need my attention immediately?"

Mister Jacobson spoke up. "I can get them home, Mister Schmidt. You can attend to the magistrate's business without delay. We will see you at supper."

Frowning, Caspar motioned for his wife and children to follow her father back to the shop and turned back to the magistrate. "What does this concern, Mister Johnson?"

Leading Caspar out of earshot of the congregants still emerging from the church, the magistrate said, "I am given to understand that you are acquainted with a Mister Sigmund Graff, late of Ewald's company of Hessians, and recently released from custody under the terms of the peace?"

Feeling the familiar clutch of fear take root between his shoulder blades, Caspar answered, "Yes. I served under him before I became separated from the company in action." He was prepared to explain the entire story to the man, but the magistrate raised a hand to stop the torrent of words.

"Very good, so you know his appearance?"

Puzzled, Caspar answered, "He was much altered by his time in captivity, but I would recognize him if I saw him, yes."

"May I ask you to come with me, then? You may be able to help me resolve a question that has been vexing me since early this morning."

"Where do you need me to go? I am but recently recovered from a terrible illness, and my strength is not what it once was."

"It's not far," Johnson said. "Just down to the mill."

Caspar nodded. "I can go that far, I think."

As they set out together, and were out of sight of the church, the magistrate said, "I must prepare you for what you will see, Mister Schmidt. I was summoned by the operator of the mill at daybreak today. He had discovered that the wheel was stopped by some obstruction, and when he diverted the flow of the water away from the raceway, he discovered that the cause of the stoppage was the body of a man."

Caspar stopped in the road. "Dead?"

"Aye. None who spend a night under the water emerge from it alive."

"And you think it was Herr Graff?"

"Someone who happened by thought that it might be that man, but said that you might know him for certain."

Caspar felt dizzy for a moment, and he bent over, resting his forearms on his knees until he regained his equilibrium. "This is news I had not looked for," he said. "I was not on good terms with the man, but I did not wish him an ill fortune."

The magistrate hurried to say, "No one made any accusations against you. As you say, you have been too ill to have done anyone any harm, and from what I heard, this Mister Graff had been working on arranging his own demise for some time, seeking it in the bottom of one bottle or another."

Caspar stood back up and motioned for them to continue on the path toward the mill. "That is true enough," he said. "I even gave him shelter on Christmas Eve, when he had lost his lodgings for the night, and was too deep into his cups to keep himself safe."

He gave a bitter laugh, recalling, "For my trouble, he said I had been unmanned by my wife and called me a traitor. I must confess that I sent him on his way with a bruise on his face in the shape of my hand. I have not seen him since."

The magistrate looked over at him with an appraising expression. "You were, if anything, restrained, sir. I think that if a man had made such comments after spending a night under my roof, I might have given him more than a bruise by which to remember his manners."

He shrugged. "If this is your Mister Graff, then you may consider the score firmly settled." The two men trudged on in silence until the mill came into view, with a knot of men gathered near the riverside.

Caspar did not know what he expected to feel when he walked over to look upon the face of the pitiable corpse laid on the muddy ground beside the mill's raceway. Gazing at the dead man, he noticed the wheel was back in operation, and the rhythmic splash of water combined with the creak of the workings inside the mill to provide a backdrop to the sight before him.

Mostly, he just felt sad that any man had met his end in such an ignominious manner. Awareness of the waste of potential represented by the broken and still form before him left Caspar thinking about the contrast between the industry of the machine in the background and the corpse's silence.

Although it was bloated from its time in the water, and bearing a gash across his forehead, there could be no doubt about it. He looked up at the magistrate and nodded confirmation. The dead man before Caspar was his old sergeant, Sigmund Graff.

Chapter 23

It felt good to be back at work, his needle darting through pliant cloth and shaping clothing for customers who had ensured that his family had a roof over their heads and food on their table.

Even though the light lasted longer with each passing day, Caspar had to lay aside his work and rest by early afternoon. Not only did his exertions tire him more quickly than ever before in his life, but his back was prone to seizing up in agonizing knots more readily that it used to be.

Today, his back was behaving itself, but the bone-deep weariness that drove him to nap before dinner most days was already setting in. As satisfying as it was to watch the tidy, even stitches build up into a straight, tight seam, he decided to finish sewing together the two panels of fabric spread across his legs, and then go back upstairs and rest.

His customers were willing to be patient with him, and the sad fate of Sergeant Graff had given him a new determination to treasure the time that he had with his family. The best way to do that was to ensure that he did not drive himself so hard that he sacrificed his health.

Mister Canter had declared himself pleased with Caspar's recovery, but had cautioned him to listen to the calls of his body for rest. While the doctor had seen no cases of lockjaw return once passed, he warned Caspar that the imbalance in the humours could be unpredictable, if it were not attended to.

"A body that has been so far unbalanced as yours was may be restored, but it will likely be more susceptible to future disturbances. However, careful attention to the body's signals of excesses in one or more of the humours may save you from falling into such a state again."

Caspar wasn't sure that he fully understood the principles behind the learned man's claims, but he was happy enough to have the imprimatur of philosophical reason to justify taking his rest when he felt called upon to do so.

Setting the work aside, he climbed down carefully and deliberately from the sewing table. Even though he still kept his feet unshod for cleanliness on his work surface, he was no longer careless about what might wait for them on the floor. His eyes moved over the floor in cautious, scanning sweeps until he was satisfied that there were no dropped pins lurking.

He barred the door, gave the cat a friendly stroke between his ears, and made his way upstairs. Karin was working on changing Lena's clothing, saying to her, "You must tell Mama when you need to go to the privy the next time. It is only a few steps down through the back door, but it takes a moment to get there."

"Yes, Mama," came Lena's high-pitched reply. "But what if a monster is there when you take me?"

Caspar paused on his way to his bed to hear this, and Karin asked, "What monsters?"

Lena sighed in an exaggerated manner. "Bjorn said not to tell you he had warned me about them, but he said that there are monsters that hide in the privy, waiting to pinch you when you sit down."

Karin's face was a study in patient frustration as she closed her eyes and visibly counted to ten in Swedish before calling out, "Bjorn, would you come here, please?"

Caspar smiled in spite of himself and shook his head, catching Karin's eye. He blew her a kiss and continued toward their bed, dodging their son as he came running in answer to his mother's no-nonsense tone.

Settling himself down to rest, Caspar could hear his wife testily informing Bjorn that if he told his sister any more tall tales about bottoms being pinched in the privy, he would get his bottom warmed in the kitchen. "There is enough for me to wash every day, without having to add more sets of your sister's clothes because you have made her afraid to use the facilities like a grown-up," she concluded.

He heard the boy's mumbled answer, and wrapped the blanket around himself, ready to sink into a peaceful slumber for the afternoon. All was well within the walls of his home, and he was grateful for his good fortune.

The back-and-forth conversation between Karin and the children served as a lullaby for his weary mind as he drifted off, secure in the knowledge that she had them well in hand.

As peaceful as his entry into sleep had been, his slumber did not remain so for long. It had been years since he had dreamed about that day at the bridge, under fire from the American ambush.

The autumn gold of the trees on the surrounding hillsides had seemed like a beckoning invitation to a boy who knew that only poverty awaited him at the end of this service, and as the company marched along, Caspar wondered idly what wealth must lie in a countryside where the very trees shone with the color of riches.

What little he had seen of the enemy didn't much reflect wealth. Their uniforms were shabby and often even mismatched, and he'd heard it said that they often fired only two or three volleys in a battle, in order to conserve precious powder and balls.

The farms and villages they had marched through seemed solidly constructed, but they were rarely ostentatious. Practicality seemed to be the order of the day here in America, although the exceptions were remarkable to see.

A shouted command from Sergeant Graff interrupted his thoughts. "Correct your formation, men! Are we a herd of cattle or professional soldiers? The captain tells me that there is a bridge up ahead, and we know that the enemy likes to use such places to their advantage, as we cannot easily pass elsewhere. Keep a sharp eye out and check that your charges are ready."

Strangely, the sergeant's face was already bloated with the mark of his far-off fate, but the gash across his forehead did not bleed, nor did the man seem to be aware of his state at all.

They came over top of the small rise that had concealed the bridge from their line of sight, and as soon as the last of the company had started down the slope, the banks of the stream to either side of the bridge had erupted in odd puffs of smoke. The sight was almost immediately followed by the sounds of the enemy's first volley claiming its victims among the company of dragoons, and, finally, by the popping sound of musket fire.

This was the point in the dream where things went one of two ways, Caspar was dimly aware. Either he would relive his shameful flight from the battle, or else he would join those already writing on the ground with injuries.

This time, though, there was the anguished scream of a woman somewhere nearby, and as he cast about to locate the source of the sound, he realized it was not a part of the familiar dream at all, but some intrusion from the waking world.

He sat bolt upright in his bed and threw off the covers, hurrying into the kitchen. Karin was at the back door, looking out over the courtyard between their house and the ones that lined the next street over, behind the shop.

The woman's scream had transitioned into loud, hoarse sobbing, and Caspar went to stand beside his wife at the doorway. Looking out, he at once understood why she was frozen at the top of the stairs.

Missus van Dusen was crouched in the muddy grass between the rows of buildings, and the wails that she was emitting were the worst sound he had heard since the day of the battle at the bridge.

Clutched in her arms was a small, crumpled form, dressed in a pale blue gown, with a shock of long, dark hair spilling out over its collar.

Karin whispered, in a stunned tone, "It is Betje. She must have fallen from the window."

Caspar wrapped his arm around her shoulder, saying only, "*Lieber Gott.*"

Chapter **24**

Trying to explain to Bjorn that his former adversary and sometimes playmate was gone forever was only one of the challenges that Caspar faced over the days that followed. Although the boy had heard of deaths before—usually babies, or the mothers of friends lost in childbirth—this was the first time that someone he had known relatively well had passed into the next life.

"Won't she have a hard time breathing inside that box, Papa?" Bjorn sat on the deep windowsill beside his father, but Caspar blocked him from getting too close to the edge with an arm stretched across to the other side of the window. He frowned, thinking that the boy's whisper must be audible all the way down on the street, as they watched the procession on its way to the Dutch church pass below.

Willem and Anke van Dusen had donned black clothes, though it appeared to Caspar's practiced eye they were particularly ill-fitting, probably borrowed for the occasion. Missus van Dusen's skirts had been made for a much taller woman, and Willem's cloak for a shorter man.

"No, son, she breathes no more," Caspar said quietly. "The dead do not breathe, nor do their hearts stir. Death is unlike sleep in these regards. Those who have died will never awaken again in this world, but their spirits have gone on to the next, where they keep company with God."

"Even someone who is mean to other people, like Betje is? I thought that Pastor Lundqvist said that people who choose to do bad things will not get to meet God."

Caspar sighed, but answered evenly, "I do not think that God would judge a little girl as harshly as he would a grown-up." Lena stood by his legs at the window, and he reached down to caress the top of her head as he spoke.

Bjorn thought about that for a while, his brows beetled in concentration. "Do you think God would judge a little boy more than a little girl? That doesn't seem fair, but you are always telling me I must do the right thing, and that God can see whenever I do something wrong."

Caspar frowned, unsure just how he had gotten himself backed into this rhetorical corner by a boy of barely five years.

Karin spoke up then, from where she stood at the other window that had a view of the street. "Perhaps you can ask Pastor Lundqvist about it on Sunday."

Bjorn seemed satisfied with that, saying, "All right, I will. I hope he tells me that Betje is banished from heaven. I do not want to find her there when I die."

Caspar found himself suddenly caught up in a coughing fit as he tried to conceal the utterly impious laughter that threatened to burst from his mouth.

Karin admonished her son gently, "Bjorn, we should never wish that upon anyone. We should hope that all the people in our lives come to know Jesus and that through knowing Him, they find grace and learn to be better versions of themselves."

Recovering himself, Caspar added, "Remember that even those who do not go immediately to heaven will have a chance at grace before the end." He frowned. "At least, I think that's how it works. Pastor Lundqvist can explain it better than I can."

Karin nodded, looking fondly over at him. "I believe you are correct, my dear, but the pastor can certainly give you the details."

Bjorn was focused now on the last of the procession as the mourners disappeared around the corner. Hopping down from the windowsill, he asked, "Mama, is there any more of that porridge left? I am hungry again."

Karin turned away from the window to take care of their son, but Caspar sat on the windowsill, gathering Lena into his arms. Children were so fragile, and their lives so fraught. Disease, accidents, and just pure bad luck conspired to keep so many of them from reaching adulthood, and Caspar could not imagine how he could survive losing one of theirs.

No matter what differences he and Willem van Dusen might have had in the past, Caspar felt nothing but compassion for the man now. His wife might take it harder than he did—which was only natural, as mothers bore their babies for nine months before fathers ever got to know them—but Willem did not deserve to suffer such a loss.

The contrast between Betje's death and Sergeant Graff's was also sharp in Caspar's mind. Based on the accounts that Caspar had heard, the girl had ignored her mother and leaned against the window in their kitchen, not knowing that Missus van Dusen had unlatched it to clear the air after a pot of stew had burned.

Although the child was perhaps willful, she could no more held responsible for the accident that had claimed her life than could her mother. Caspar knew that Missus van Dusen must be wracked with self-recrimination anyway, but it was clear to him, at least, that it had been a tragic accident, and nothing more.

Sergeant Graff, on the other hand, had taken an active and ongoing role in his own destruction. Although it would never be certain how he had come to be in the millrace, most people assumed he had stumbled and fallen in, while yet again under the influence of strong drink.

Given the number of times that the man had been seen drunk, there was a sense of inevitability that it would lead to his end. The precise mechanism by which he met his Maker was only of mild interest. He had set himself on that path over and over again.

Betje, for all of her childish misbehavior, was not an inherently bad person, and her fate had resulted from a single careless moment, not a repeated tempting of chance.

Pastor Lundqvist might have some wisdom to share with them all on Sunday, and Caspar was genuinely looking forward to the services on Sunday. Attending church had seemed much less like a necessary chore and more like a welcome return to normalcy ever since his illness—and his own brush with the hereafter—but he had rarely felt as eager for it as he did now.

Being able to turn over all of his own questions and confusion to the authority of the pastor's greater acquaintance with the word and deeds of the Lord was very appealing in a moment such as this. And, of course, giving Bjorn a chance to resolve his own curiosity would be good, as well.

Lena chose this moment to twist around in Caspar's embrace, turning to face him with a solemn expression on her face. "Papa?"

"Yes, Lena?"

"Is Bet-leh . . . Bet-je," she corrected herself, pronouncing the girl's name carefully and deliberately, "never coming back?"

"No, Lena, she is never coming back"

She sat for a moment, thinking, and then said, "That makes me sad and happy at the same time. I am happy that we will not have to stay away from her anymore, but I am sad for her mama."

"I am sad for her mama, too," Caspar said, and placed a gentle kiss on the toddler's forehead. "And even though her papa and I do not get along, I am sad for him as well."

Lena nodded. "I don't like him. But he should not have to say bye to Bet-je, either." She snuggled into Caspar's chest, and he cherished the wiggly, warm presence there, until she could no longer stay still, and hopped down to go see what her mother was doing in the kitchen with Bjorn.

Caspar stayed seated at the windowsill, watching the few passers-by going about their ordinary business below. Their lives went on unaltered by the tragedy that had befallen one of their neighbors. Caspar's thoughts turned to the trials he had faced, and to the strangely wonderful revelations it had brought, as he had discovered just how deeply valued he was in the community.

He had known, of course, that his dedicated customers appreciated the quality of his work, but without his illness, he might never had discovered the high esteem with which they regarded him as a person. Though he would never have chosen to suffer the bout of lockjaw, he was still grateful for it, in a way, because of what it had made him see of his value to the entire community.

He wondered whether Willem van Dusen would experience a similar discovery, despite his abrasive personality and foolishness in clinging to a past that was gone, never to return. Those who agreed with him, of course, would be more inclined to support him in his time of need, but was a mere disagreement over politics enough to withhold the recognition of the man's loss?

What of past conflicts, then? Or resentments born of childhood misunderstandings? Did those make van Dusen's loss any less acute, or any less real? He had, in his own way, obviously loved his daughter, and wanted a bright future for her, regardless of what he thought was most likely to bring about such a future.

Caspar recalled the people whose support had most surprised him in his illness, when Karin had told him about them. Most of those who had taken part in the attempt to shun him after Graff's arrival and the rumors that the old soldier had tried to spread about him seemed to have felt remorse for their actions, and had been among the most generous of their neighbors.

The prospect of Caspar being claimed by the illness which had struck him seemed to have driven them to acts of kind charity, as they realized they did not seek that outcome.

The van Dusens had not been among those who had brought food or business, of course, although Willem arguably had greater responsibility for Caspar falling ill than anyone else in the community. If he had not stormed out of the shop, slamming the door and scattering the pins, Caspar might well have been spared the entire ordeal.

So who would show such kindness to the van Dusens? Betje had been their only child, and with her gone, the couple had only one another to depend upon. Caspar could not see how he might offer the man any kindness, without it being seen as a craven attempt to take advantage of van Dusen's misfortune.

Still, the truth of the matter was that his heart was not unmoved by the man's loss. If there were some way to acknowledge it without the man taking it the wrong way, he could not think of it. It seemed unbearable to let the man's loss go unacknowledged, though.

Then it struck him. The van Dusens had need of mourning clothes that would fit them over the next year, and he could supply them out of the stock he had on hand.

Chapter 25

Caspar did not need to take measurements for either of the van Dusens to produce garments that were a better fit for them than were the borrowed items. While bespoke clothing would always fit best, it was utterly impossible to ask them to come in to his shop. Willem's pride and Anke's grief would have stood in the way, and Caspar intended to simply deliver the clothes without attribution, so that neither he nor Willem would need to acknowledge it publicly.

Cutting and seaming the black cloth, using thread dyed to match, was a challenge for even an eye as practiced as Caspar's, but his needle flew through the work almost without pause, even for his own needs.

He'd told Karin of his intentions, and she had said only, "It is a worthy gesture, my dear, and I know Willem will appreciate it, even if he cannot say so. As for his wife, well, she will probably be insensate to such mundane details for the time being, but in time, she will also probably be touched by it."

She had reached out to touch Caspar's face. "Are you doing this out of a sense of guilt for the harsh words that have passed between you and Willem? This horrible event was in no conceivable way your doing, even if you had wished him or his daughter ill."

He sighed. "I do not believe that I suffer guilt, but only compassion for the man. Whatever our history may be—whatever your history with him may be—no man deserves to have to bury his only child. Oh, I know it happens to many, but children are rarely taken with no warning like this."

Shaking his head and frowning, he said, "Perhaps I am driven to do this because of my guilt at having fought with him on various occasions, and for the uncharitable thoughts I have entertained within my own mind about his daughter. While I did not wish her joy, neither did I wish her dead. It is complex, in truth, but I feel that this is the right thing for me to do."

She nodded. "I understand. I have never gotten to know Anke, since Willem found her, but she does not appear she to be a bad person. She listens to her husband, of course, as a wife ought to, and so she may have formed opinions about us that are unwarranted, but I do not think that she would refuse a gift such as this given in good faith."

Caspar had then told Karin of his intention to deliver the clothing without calling on the van Dusens. "They will doubtless understand who has brought the package, but requiring them to look me in the eye and attempt to feign gratitude would be only self-serving. It will be enough for me to see them abroad in town wearing mourning clothes that do not make a mockery of their grief."

"This is kinder by far than I had understood at first. My dear, you had wondered aloud at the kindness and support we received in our time of need, and asked why our neighbors would have done this. You asked what you might have done to deserve such love from friends and casual acquaintances."

She kissed the tip of his nose. "This is the sort of thing that they were thinking of, Caspar. You have a knack for doing the right thing, even when it would be far easier to simply do nothing at all. People notice it, and it makes them care for you."

Caspar grumbled good-naturedly, "I have done these things less often than you all seem to give me credit for, but it is fine to be seen that way, I suppose."

Sitting on the sewing table with the heavy wool of Willem's new cloak spread over his legs, Caspar thought about what good actions that man had taken, what might cause the community to fly to his aid in the crisis.

As the keeper of a shabby older inn in the Dutch part of town, van Dusen had doubtless made more than his share of enemies over the years. The work of dealing with men who did not know their capacity for strong drink, with travelers who did not know the limits of their purses, and with all manner of petty thieves and unsavory characters, it was impossible that he had not found himself at odds with many such people over the years.

At the same time, a man who could keep a business like that as a going concern through the throes of a war must have had some friends, people who offered him terms when he didn't really deserve them, who gave him business when his accommodations were not really to their taste, and so on. Too, he would have had opportunities to show leniency with his less desirable clientele, and that would have garnered him friends as well.

However, the man's natural unpleasantness meant that many who might otherwise have been driven to help him after this tragedy would simply turn their backs on him. After all, it had been difficult for Caspar to justify doing anything but that.

His church, of course, and the Loyalist community, what there might be of it, would have been moved to help him, but there were—to Caspar's knowledge—few enough in either of those communities that the man might have relatively few true friends to rely upon.

His personal unpleasantness did not reduce his human loss, though, and so Caspar stitched and trimmed, and continued working on the project. The cloak would be finished before the end of the day, and the skirt would take only a few hours' more worth of finishing work.

He'd had to set the project aside for a day in favor of a pressing seam repair for a paying client, but once he had completed that work, he'd been able to turn back to the van Dusen's garments. Perhaps by the time he needed to stop working tomorrow, he would have them complete.

Karin came down the stairs quietly and walked over to stand behind him, resting her hand on his shoulder. He rarely liked to have anyone watch him work—it reminded him too much of working under his master's critical eye during his apprenticeship—but today, it felt to him more like she was taking part in the job of doing a decent thing for a neighbor.

He finished the seam he had been working on and leaned back to rest his head against her shoulder. She said, "It is fine work that you are doing for Willem. I do hope that he appreciates its quality, whether or not he appreciates its source."

He smiled to himself and answered, "Few men can see the difference between work that is done just well enough and work that is given the extra care of a true craftsman. They are left to discover it after wearing a garment for months or even years, when they might notice that one piece is still nearly as sound as it was on the day that they got it, and another has fallen to rags."

"I think that some must be able to tell the different, else why would they pay for the work of the craftsman?"

"I have made my reputation on my work fitting clients better than what they could acquire elsewhere, as well as being current with the fashions as they develop, and, of course, lasting better than most anything they might stitch together themselves."

He leaned forward again and shrugged, looking over his shoulder at her. "Even all of that is only enough to convince some people that my work is worth paying for, as you know. Some make their own clothes, using such cloth as they can find in the market, and others rely on handed-down articles."

"Yes, my dear. I suppose that what I meant was that you win enough business that there are men who can discern the quality of your work, even if they cannot name the exact elements that set it apart."

Caspar reached up and took Karin's hand where it still rested on his shoulder. "I cannot complain about the amount of business that I have, when there is a waiting list for my services that will last for months yet."

He turned again and gave her a rueful smile. "Longer than that, even, when I can but work a few hours in a day before I must rest. I will finish adding the clasps on this cloak and then come upstairs for the night, I think."

"I do not mean to hurry you through your work, Caspar. I only wanted to see how you were doing, given how much Willem's loss affected you."

"I think I was not the only one who was affected," he said. "He was your friend for many years, long before he became my foe. Part of what moved me to do this work was to honor that friendship, even in its breach."

Karin answered slowly, "I had not considered the matter in that light. My friendship with him once meant a lot to me, even if it meant something different to him in the end. I esteem what you are doing even more now."

She thought for a moment, and then added quietly, "I am glad that you explained this to me, as it has settled in my mind the worry that I have had over whether you feared he might be a rival for my affections."

"I never—" Caspar began, but she silenced him with a finger across his lips.

"I know you said nothing to express such a fear, but it was in my mind that you might have harbored thoughts of that kind. It would be entirely natural for a man to do so, on hearing that his wife had once had another suitor before him. When you told me you wanted to do this for Willem and Anke, it made me very happy, but I did not understand why until now."

She bent and kissed the top of his head. "Seeing you work on this project is the most tangible evidence I could have asked for that you have never worried about my past affection for Willem. It is a statement not only of your decency as a neighbor, but of your trust in me, and I am grateful for both."

Chapter 26

The day had been clear and cold, which meant that Caspar could undertake his clandestine delivery with no fear that the package would be spoiled by rain. The two finished garments were wrapped in plain paper, without any label or note, and he tucked the parcel under his arm as he donned his own cloak.

He called upstairs to tell Karin he was going out and stepped into the brisk springtime afternoon. He thought that there might yet be frost overnight and was glad to see that most of the trees had not yet risked opening their buds.

A stretch of sunny days had left the streets hard-packed and relatively dry, and he walked slowly, savoring the signs of spring's rebirth that were visible. Alongside the road, the snowdrops raised their delicate stems, white blossoms modestly bowing from their low crowns. They were joined here and there by the more exuberant purple of crocuses, which opened brazenly to welcome in whatever bees might be flying this early in the year.

Although he rarely stopped to notice flowers, there was something about the appearance of these that always cheered him after the dreary, dark days of the winter. This year, in particular, the reminder of the many little joys of having weathered his own dark days made him feel cheerier than he could recall being in months, perhaps even years.

He puzzled over this further as he made his way through the

alley where he could cross over to the street behind his. Although he still did not celebrate Graff's demise, he could not deny that life without constant anxiety that he might be denounced further at any moment was less worrisome.

For that matter, he doubted that van Dusen would have any inclination to make further trouble for him any time in the foreseeable future, either. Relief from that worry had come by a means that Caspar would never have wished for, but he could not ignore the fact that the tragedy had, in fact, come with some measure of relief.

Emerging from the alley onto the street where van Dusen's inn stood, he was surprised to find the man walking slowly toward him, his head bent low, and the ill-fitting mourning cloak pulled tightly around himself. Caspar thought he had never seen such a portrait of despair, but he did not want to risk a confrontation with the target of his charity. He turned around abruptly and went back into the alley, determined to wait for a better time to make his delivery.

His hope that the other man might not have noticed him was dashed when his face appeared at the entrance of the alleyway, and he called out in a low, dispirited tone, "Mister Schmidt. I did not expect to see you out and about so soon after your illness. You do not need to run from me; I am no danger to any man in these days."

Caspar replied evenly, "I did not turn away out of fear of you, Mister van Dusen, but out of a desire to respect your grief and leave you in peace with it. I cannot imagine how you feel, but despite our differences in the past, I do not wish to add to your burthens."

An expression of mild surprise came over van Dusen's face, and he nodded slowly. "I thank you for your consideration, and for the sentiment, sir. You may continue with whatever business brought you this way without fear of causing me any distress. I am but taking a turn about the neighborhood to clear my head."

He bowed listlessly and continued up the street, disappearing from view. The man's carriage and words worried Caspar almost more than had the prospect of an encounter with him. He seemed even more affected by his loss than Caspar had guessed, and as he emerged from the alley again, he glanced down the street to van Dusen's retreating form.

He shook his head sadly to himself and decided to go ahead with the intended objective of his own walk around the neighborhood. Approaching the front step of the inn, he bent and set down his package with as much nonchalance as he could muster, and then continued on his way to the end of the block, where he turned back toward his own street.

The encounter with van Dusen left him feeling even more compassion for the man, and he was hopeful from the tone of their conversation that he and his wife might receive his gift without misunderstanding its intent.

Back at his own door, he took another deep breath of the early springtime air before entering to return to the work he had set aside for the mourning clothes. He already had the cloth cut out for two pairs of breeches for Missus Martyn's son—"He grows out of them every six months, it seems"—for which she had insisted on depositing the whole price. It felt good to have loyal customers, and better yet when they found excuses to ensure that Karin and the children were provided for.

Where most customers were perfectly satisfied with buttons of iron or even brass, she had asked that the breeches be made with buttons covered in cloth matching the fabric of the garment itself. It was an affectation that Caspar thought might be short-lived, and it made for fussy, detailed work, but she had not balked at the cost.

"Georg must be presentable, Mister Schmidt. After all, he is to accompany his father to Philadelphia this summer, and one never knows who he might meet there."

Caspar was focused on gathering and stitching cloth over the brass forms when he saw movement through the window. Mister Phillips stood looking at the door, as though unsure whether he should enter. Caspar put one stitch through the cloth to hold it in place and then rose to open the door.

Phillips saw him stand, and stepped back, clasping his hands behind his back to wait as Caspar opened the door.

"Mister Phillips, this is an unexpected pleasure. Please, come inside where it is warm, and let us talk."

The man seemed ill at ease, but he nodded and came into the shop. "Mister Schmidt, I am most gratified to see you well again." He paused as Caspar closed the door, his eyes roving about the room and seeming to avoid Caspar's.

Abruptly, the man turned to face Caspar and said, "Willem van Dusen has had an accident, and although he seems likely to make a recovery, his wife asked me to come and speak to you."

Caspar gasped, "What has happened to him?"

"He was walking along the top of the quarry, and he must have slipped, for he fell over the side. By good fortune, he landed not on rock, but in a pool of water that happened to have gathered where he fell, and he was able to get himself out and return home."

Caspar sat heavily on the stool by the hearth, and motioned for Phillips to take a seat, as well. His landlord did so, continuing, "I believe that Mister Canter attended you in your illness, did he not? He has examined Mister van Dusen and found that the man broken his arm and his collarbone, besides the many bruises and scrapes one might expect to accumulate in such a fall."

"But why did his wife send you to speak with me?" Caspar had a premonition that his act of charity might have been misinterpreted after all.

"Someone brought in a packet that had been left at their door, and in it was clothing that appeared to be of new manufacture, although there was nothing to say where it had come from. She thought that you might have made it."

"I did," Caspar acknowledged, "though it was of my own accord, and I did not intend to ask acknowledgment or even take credit for having done so. I was moved to an act of charity for people who had suffered an unimaginable loss."

"She wished me to discover whether you had made the clothes, and whether you might reveal who had commissioned the work from you, if you had."

Phillips gave Caspar a shrewd look, and added, "I did not expect to learn that you had done the work without commission, I will confess, given your history with Mister van Dusen. He exerted himself quite energetically against the arrangement that you and I made, and he had hoped to disadvantage you—even ruin you—as a consequence of my father's death."

He frowned in remembered uncertainty, saying, "I have never developed a clear understanding of his reasons for wanting to do so, other than his little-disguised sentiment toward the Crown in the late war. He seemed to regard you as having acted against that interest, although my father noted often to me you had no history of being a partisan on either side of the conflict that he was aware of."

"I believe he had learned that I once was a Hessian soldier, under contract through my landgrave in my childhood home to fight with the British forces here in America. I left that service long ago through an accident, but Mister van Dusen had concluded without evidence that I had turned traitor against my officers."

"That explains much," Phillips said, with a brisk nod. "May I ask what brought you to undertake this project without compensation?"

Caspar drew a deep breath, and decided that he must place his trust in the young man's judgment, even if he were here on Missus van Dusen's behalf.

"My conscience would not permit me to observe the terrible events that befell the van Dusen family without being moved. I recalled the many acts of charity from which I benefited in my illness, and remembered how many of them had been offered by men whose enmity toward me I had thought unshakable."

He shrugged. "Despite the face that Willem van Dusen had not been among those to extend an olive branch of care toward me in my need, and had instead been the original reason that I found myself in need, when I saw the two of them in their misfitted mourning clothes, I knew I had it in my power to right this small part of the wrong done to them by malevolent fate."

Phillips frowned, evidently trying to understand what Caspar was telling him. "But would you not want the objects of your benevolence to know that you were trying to bridge the differences between you?"

Caspar spread his hands helplessly. "I thought it might appear I were using their misfortune to win their friendship, and that was not my intention at all. As Missus van Dusen has done, I thought they might detect that I had done the work, and I did not want them to feel any obligation to feel gratitude toward me. Such an obligation has a tendency to turn into resentment."

Phillips set his hands upon his knees and tipped his head back in thought. "I believe that it might have done that, save for Mister van Dusen's newest misfortune. Between you and me, I am not certain that it was an accident at all, as everyone who knows him is acquainted with the depths of his despair following his daughter's death."

The thought sent a shock through Caspar's mind, and he said, "Oh, no, I do not believe that of him. He seemed burthened, but not beyond bearing, when I saw him this afternoon."

Phillips looked sharply at him. "You saw the man this afternoon?"

"Yes, and in fact, I believe it must have been as he was setting out for the walk that would bring him to the quarry. By happenstance, he was on his way down the street from his door as I was approaching with my package. His appearance there took me by surprise, but he seemed in solemn spirits, and not in a state of irretrievable despair."

"I am heartened to hear that," Phillips said. "A man who is intent upon self-destruction may be given different treatment than one who is merely prone to self-destructive error. Steps can be taken to dissuade intentional acts, but I suppose that there is little that can be done to protect a man whose mind is distracted from the necessities of self-preservation."

He shrugged. "I do not believe that Mister van Dusen is likely to be in a position again to come to self-destructive harm for quite some time, whether intentional or accidental, though. So while the coincidence that you encountered him shortly before his accident is interesting, I do not believe that it is likely to change what his physician finds necessary in his treatment."

Standing, he bowed to Caspar. "With your permission, I will confirm to Missus van Dusen that you are the maker of their new mourning clothes, but if you prefer, I will say only that their benefactor prefers to remain unnamed."

Caspar rose from his own seat and said, "I believe that is for the best. Thank you for your care. I will pray for Mister van Dusen's recovery, and for comfort for both of them."

Chapter 27

As had happened before, Willem van Dusen came to the door of Caspar's shop. This time, however, wrapped in his new cloak, he knocked and waited for Caspar to answer. Although he was surprised to see him, and perhaps more surprised at the difference in the man's bearing since the last time he'd encountered him, Caspar said, "Mister van Dusen, I heard of your accident, and I did not expect to see you about so soon. Please, come in."

It was, at least, a warmer day today, but the warmth of the hearth still made for an improvement over the cool air flowing in through the doorway. Caspar motioned van Dusen toward the comfortable wooden chair and took the stool for himself. "What brings you to my shop, sir?"

The other man sat, his cloak opening to reveal his arm bound against his chest. He gave Caspar a weary-looking gaze, and said quietly, "Let us not pretend, Mister Schmidt, that I am ignorant of where this cloak came from. I would like to thank you for the quality and speed of your work."

Caspar acknowledged van Dusen's praise with a nod of his head, but the man continued, "I should like to satisfy my curiosity as to who persuaded you to undertake this work, despite the differences of opinion that you and I have had in the past. I have been . . . unkind to you in the past, and I can appreciate that performing a service such as this for me in light of that must have given you pause."

At first, Caspar was inclined to continue his claim that an anonymous benefactor had asked him to make the cloak and skirt, but looking into van Dusen's tired eyes, he decided instead to tell the whole truth.

"Mister van Dusen, whatever had passed between us before meant nothing when I witnessed your wife wailing over your little girl's body. As one father to another, I could not hold my hurt above yours, and when I noted that you wanted for proper mourning clothes, I saw that I could do something that might ease your burthens, if only by the least amount."

The other man's eyebrows shot up as he leaned forward, and his face showed the most animation that Caspar had seen on it since Betje's death. "You . . . commissioned yourself to do this work?"

Caspar said, soberly, "I did, yes."

Mister van Dusen sank back in his chair, regarding Caspar with an inscrutable expression on his face for a long moment. Finally, he said quietly, "I should have come by when you were ill, Mister Schmidt. I considered it, but thought better of it when I reflected on how we left things when last we spoke. I did not believe that I would be welcome under your roof."

Caspar nodded in agreement. "In truth, sir, you might have found a chilly reception. I do not know if you were aware of this, but it is likely that the lockjaw resulted from being stuck in the foot by a pin that fell when you closed the door after yourself that day."

Van Dusen's look of horror as he realized what Caspar was telling him seemed utterly sincere. "I did not know! I never intended to do you harm, no matter how much disdain I might have convinced myself to feel for you." He dropped his face into his free hand and his shoulders quaked as though he might be weeping.

When he looked up again, his eyes were red-rimmed, and he added, "If only because of my eternal regard for Karin, and my hope that she should find joy, I would never truly wish harm upon the man she loves."

He met Caspar's eyes, and said, "Now, I am doubly sorry that my ill-considered actions brought you to such a grave pass, sir. You have shown yourself to be ten times the man I am, and I am ashamed to ever have spoken so cruelly to you."

Caspar scoffed, "Nonsense, Mister van Dusen. If the only evidence I had was found in Karin's friendship with you when you were youths, I should consider that sufficient to show that you are a decent man. Even very good men may be led astray, as we know too well. As for those of us who are made of mere clay? Well, it is enough that we should seek to do right when an opportunity is presented to us."

He gestured at the cloak. "I have done no more than that in making mourning clothes for you and Missus van Dusen. If I had failed to meet this opportunity, why then, I should have thought as little of myself as you once did. Do you see that?"

Van Dusen nodded slowly. "I think so, yes." He closed his eyes, pain etched over his face, and said, "I only wish that we had not had to suffer such a loss to have learned your true quality."

With all the sincerity in his heart, Caspar said, "I wish you had not had to lose your daughter at all, sir. I know that there is nothing I can say or do that will make that tragedy any easier to bear. I know you doted upon her, and I knew her only slightly."

He paused and asked, "Would you tell me about Betje, if you can? It may be well to remember her to me."

"I think I can bear to speak about her a little, yes." He paused, and then began, "When Anke and I were courting, what we wanted more than anything else in the world was to have children together. She had always dreamed of having a full house, and when I inherited the inn, I thought it would be possible to support as many as she could want."

He shook his head sadly, more pain etched upon his face. "While she was with child after we married, she was happier than I had ever seen her before. I would come into the kitchen to find her murmuring to our baby, singing sometimes, and even dancing, though she was great with child."

Caspar smiled, remembering Karin's pregnancies differing somewhat from this, but van Dusen continued, "She delivered the baby with only the normal amount of difficulty, and at first, all seemed to be well. However, two days after Betje was born, Anke developed a terrible fever. The midwife said something about her not having been completely delivered of the afterbirth, but in truth, I remember little of that time."

He looked up bleakly at Caspar. "I thought for certain that I was going to lose them both, because we could find no one who could nurse the baby while Anke was ill, and even after my wife recovered, her milk had gone, and Betje suffered terribly. This was well after the war had started, and everything was in short supply."

Caspar said, "I think it must have been right around the time when I arrived here, because I remember hearing that one of the women who worked at the public house where I first lived here had gone to nurse a child whose mother had lost her milk to a fever."

"Yes, probably. It was a hardship for us all, naturally, but Anke felt it particularly, because not only did she lose the ability to nurse her own child, but the midwife told her she would never have another."

Fresh tears sprang to the man's eyes, and he said, "You must know that this history makes our loss of Betje all the harder to bear. She was so much wished for, and fought for, and for her to be lost like this . . . well, I don't know how we will ever survive."

Caspar said nothing, because he knew that his experience offered nothing that could be of any comfort. He felt that the best thing he could do for van Dusen was simply to hear his story. He said, gently, "Betje seemed to have grown into a normal child in every respect that I could see."

"Oh, yes, once we found a nurse for her, she grew up like a weed springing from the earth. She was strong and healthy, and willful, even as a tiny child."

A small smile passed across his face, and he said, "She could be a real trial for us sometimes. As soon as she learned to walk, she would put anything she could reach into her mouth. One time, I am fairly certain that she swallowed an entire guinea—it went missing from my desk, and I never saw it again. It is lucky that it did not choke her."

He shook his head in remembered regret. "Oh, I raged about that guinea, as I needed it to pay a bill, but she never admitted to having touched it. In truth, I should have kept it out of her reach."

He buried his face in his hand again and sobbed aloud. Caspar heard his muffled cry, "Oh, I would give a hundred guineas to just hold my little girl again!"

Catching movement out of the corner of his eye, Caspar saw Karin looking curiously down into the shop, her eyes widening when she recognized who was there with him. He motioned her back upstairs with a toss of his head, and she nodded silently as she retreated. He would tell her everything later, but he felt certain that van Dusen would not want any additional witnesses to his pain.

Van Dusen visibly regained control over himself, and then continued. "In truth, I scolded her rarely, because I was most of the time simply so grateful to have her." Caspar said nothing, but thought privately that this had been his entire problem with the child.

"But, in truth, it wasn't very often that she needed scolding, for all that she was sometimes trying. She knew that she could have what she wanted from us most times, and we were happy to give her whatever we could, knowing that she would never have brothers or sisters."

He shrugged, and concluded, "Now that she is gone, there seems little left to look forward to in this life. Hard work, old age, infirmity, and the release of death, and nothing to show for it all."

Caspar said firmly, "Not at all, sir. You will have your influence on those around you to show for everything you do. A man's legacy is not confined only to his issue, else some of the greatest figures of history should be disregarded for never having added to this groaning world's burthens."

The other man looked up at him sharply, saying, "I am uncertain that I take your meaning."

"Consider General Washington, sir, whatever you may think of him. He has, I believe, no issue. Yet do you doubt for a moment that his legacy is secure forever?"

Van Dusen frowned, but shook his head. Leaning forward and holding his gaze, Caspar said, "You will make your mark upon the world now through your good works. The service you offer to your guests, the kindnesses that you do for your neighbors, the matters you discuss in church, those will now be your legacy, and there is no shame to be found in being remembered that way."

Van Dusen chewed on his lip and appeared to be trying to stop himself from beginning to weep again. "I think . . . I think I can live with that."

Chapter 28

Upstairs, after van Dusen had departed, with the children both sound asleep at their afternoon naps, Caspar sat down heavily at the kitchen table. "I feel as though I bear the weight of that man's soul on my shoulders."

"What on Earth were you two discussing, like old friends of close confidence?" Karin shook her head in wonder. "I have never seen Willem weep so, even when he and I had our misunderstanding."

"I think Mister van Dusen and I may have finally come to understand one another."

"After all that he has done to you—to us?" Karin seemed aghast.

"Spreading unkind rumors and accidentally spilling needles on the floor are not the actions of a friend, it is true. But neither are they unforgivable trespasses. What had passed between you and him many years ago should have been forgotten long before now. Holding anger in your heart for so long can lead to no good for anyone."

Karin spoke carefully, but Caspar could hear an edge of anger in her tone. "These are his errors, yet you speak as though you are counseling us—or even just me—about the dangers of bearing long-term grudges."

"Yes, I agree. These are the errors which have helped to

bring van Dusen much ill, and I should like for us to avoid repeating them ourselves. His present grief has no relation to anything that has gone before between us. I thought you had agreed that what I was doing in making them mourning clothes was the correct action in the circumstances."

"Oh, yes, that I believed, and still believe, was an opportunity to show to yourself and all that you are the better man, able to put aside the past and act with compassion to a man who could not bring himself to do likewise in your moment of crisis."

"He thought about doing so, but feared the reception that such an act might receive, particularly given his past with you. He did not know of his role in my illness, and that ignorance would doubtless have led to additional misunderstandings between you and him. No, I think it was well that he did not bring the olive branch at that time."

Karin scowled but said, reluctantly, "I suppose you are right. But I still do not understand how you came to be sharing confidences and sympathies in so short a time after having been foes for so long."

Caspar shrugged. "We both have been changed by events well beyond our control, and sometimes long acquaintance is of more value in finding understanding than is friendship. As I said, we finally understand one another, he and I. That is no small thing, even if we remain of different opinions on many matters."

He gazed at Karin as she visibly tried to understand what he was telling her. Gently, he added, "I believe Willem van Dusen intended to murder himself when he fell into the quarry. A man like him does not come to that point without having lost all hope that his life has mattered. By permitting him to see how his actions have affected me, I believe that I might have shown him a little bit of the broader effects that his life has had."

Karin frowned. "Does it help a man see how he has hurt others when you are trying to persuade him that his life has had meaning?"

"I believe that it just might, if only to show him that by making better choices in the future, he might effect change that he can be proud of—as well as proving to him that his errors can be forgiven, even by his fellow men, never mind by God, who forgives all."

Karin thought about this for a long moment, her brow furrowed in consideration. "I suppose I see what you are getting at, my dear."

"Do you not think that he has suffered enough in his present prostration? Karin, if you had heard him tell me of what Betje meant to him and to Missus van Dusen, if you had witnessed the depth of his grief when he spoke of their loss, I should think that your heart would have to be made of stone to not have been moved as mine was."

Karin smiled at that. "My heart is not made of stone, as you know well, and I have prayed nightly for their grief to find some solace."

"I am not sure that it can," Caspar said, and told Karin about Anke's illness after Betje's birth.

Karin nodded sadly. "I had heard that she was taken ill after the baby was born, and that he was seeking a nurse for Betje, but I did not know that her illness had left her barren. That certainly makes the child's loss all that harder to accept."

A blaze of anger rose in her eyes, though, as she added, "And how much crueler it would have been had he succeeded in what you take to have been his object in ending his life at the quarry? How was Anke to have survived that additional loss?"

Caspar shrugged. "A man who has reached the point of throwing away his own life can convince himself of the notion—that the rest of us can readily see is ridiculous—that those in his life would be happier without him. It is not even a selfish thought in them. They come to honestly believe that they can make things better for those they care about by removing themselves from this life."

Karin scowled. "It is a mortal sin to even entertain such thoughts within the privacy of one's mind. I find it curious that you are familiar with them, my husband."

He acknowledged her unstated question with a nod of his head. "I have never felt this way, but I saw men in my company fall to such depths in their despair at being away from their homes, or at the loss of companions whom they loved. We learned to be alert to the signs of such sentiments developing in the minds of those around us, so that they might be led away from the edge of their despair."

He pursed his mouth and added, sadly, "It was not always possible to discover that a man had reached that point until he had thrown himself over the side of a ship, or stood and openly exposed himself to the fire of the enemy in battle."

Sighing, he said, "Those losses could be passed off as having been the normal outcomes of the hazards of transport over seas and participation in a war, but ofttimes the man might have left a letter or some other evidence of the state of his mind that we could not deny. I learned to be vigilant for the indications, but even so, I know men whose loss I suspect could have been avoided."

Karin shook her head. "I still do not comprehend the state of mind that could lead a man to believe that his grieving wife would grieve less at two graves than at one."

"Nor do I, my dear. I am just glad that Missus van Dusen and her husband will continue to have each other to turn to for support as they try to come to terms with this new reality of theirs."

He paused for a moment and then continued, "And I think they would be well served to come to the realization that they do not stand alone in this. I can tell you from my own certain knowledge the benefit of feeling the support and love of community around oneself. It is even more wondrous when it is a community that you never suspected would be there for you, and I think that the van Dusens may be people who do not believe themselves to have a community that surrounds them."

Karin looked thoughtful. "I do not know Anke well, I will confess. We do not encounter one another in church, of course, and though we might have at various times exchanged a word or two about our children, or at the market, I cannot say that I have ever had a discussion of any meaning with her."

"Perhaps now is the time," Caspar said.

She frowned. "I am not so ready to set aside years of small slights, little sideways comments their daughter repeated to our children, never mind her husband's efforts to ruin your business, take our home from us, and his indispensable role in bringing you to the very brink of the hereafter."

Caspar gave her a small smile. "When you put it that way, it makes my willingness to do so sound like a self-destructive foolishness," he admitted. "But let me ask you this: Do you think he is likely to undertake any of those actions against us in the future, since I made that effort?"

She gave him a sour look. "No, and though it pains me to say so, you have the right of it in a sober analysis. But I am not one of those Mechanical Turks that you have told me of reading about, able to consider the next move in a game of chess with emotionless logic alone. My heart was hurt by the things that they said within Betje's hearing, and which she repeated against our children."

He reached out and took her hand. "My heart was not unhurt by their comments, either, and learning that Mister van Dusen was motivated not merely by rank prejudice or even political opinion, but by an unrequited love for you did nothing to lessen the hurt. Still, as I said before, cherishing that hurt within my heart did nothing to cure it, and neither did holding a grudge against the man who inflicted it."

Karin sighed deeply and nodded. "I will ask whether I may call on Anke once a few days have passed, out of decency. After all, they have just buried their child, and they cannot be expected to welcome guests, can they?"

"No, I do not suppose that they can, though I really only know the ways of my people and yours. Do the Dutch have some practice in this regard peculiar to them?"

"Not that I have heard about, no. But I will make discreet inquiries."

"Very good, my dear. Thank you." He put his hands on his knees and stood. "I must return to my paying commissions while my strength remains for the afternoon, lest I put my reputation and our income at risk."

Chapter 29

The full glory of spring fairly burst into view through the window as Caspar descended into his shop. The morning was bright, and the sky bore only a few cotton tufts of cloud, none of which threatened rain. Down the street, an apple tree was still in exuberant bloom, though the ground beneath it was already white with fallen petals.

Caspar crossed the room to the door and threw it open, welcoming in the clean morning air, and trying to overlook the faint addition of a passing horse's droppings in the street.

A pair of squirrels chased each other around the trunk of the apple, chittering and scolding one another. One caught the movement as Caspar turned to go back inside, and they both froze before directing their ire at him. He smiled to himself at their behavior at seeing a common foe and settled down at his sewing table.

He wanted to finish up the waistcoat for young Master Inkvist so that he could deliver the item to his father at church on Sunday. It would be yet another item he could strike off in the order log, and one less obligation pressing on him. Although his customers were, to a person, understanding of the time it was taking him to get through all the work they'd asked of him during his illness, those pages of incomplete commissions were almost more stressful than a lack of work would have been.

He smiled to himself, thinking about the unexpected growth in his clientele. After he and Willem had bridged the divide between themselves, there were nearly as many Dutch names being added to his ledger as Swedish. While the most vocal of the former Loyalists still stayed away, the less strident were drawn by his reputation for good work and kindness.

As the community had adjusted to the state of peace and American ascendancy, most Loyalists seemed to have resigned themselves to this new reality. He'd heard of old friendships being rekindled, sometimes with rueful admissions on both sides of the artificial ill-will that the national divide had fostered.

He caught motion out of the corner of his eye, and smiled broadly to see that Anke was at the doorway, still clad in the mourning dress he had made. Her face bore a tentative smile, a contrast to the weariness that still hung about her eyes. Setting his work aside, he clambered down from the table and greeted her warmly.

"Missus van Dusen, it is so good to see you abroad in the town on such a lovely day. How do you fare?"

She drew a deep breath and replied, "About as well as can be expected, Mister Schmidt. My husband asked me to inquire as to whether he might trouble you for a commission."

Caspar nodded, saying, "Nothing would make me happier, madame. What is the nature of the work he requires?"

As Anke described a set of simple curtains that needed to be replaced after a careless traveler had nearly burnt down the inn, Caspar nodded encouragingly.

When she finished by saying, "The wicked fiend departed without taking responsibility for his foolish mistake, so we must pay for these out of our own pockets," Caspar raised a hand, smiling.

"To begin with, I am most gratified to hear that the damage was not more general. Curtains are a simple matter to measure, cut, and stitch, and the cost can be kept very moderate by selecting less costly material. Have you the dimensions needed?"

She pulled a slip of paper from the pocket under her apron and handed it over. "We certainly need nothing extravagant in these difficult times. Whatever you might supply that will render the room fit to use again will be fine."

She grimaced, and added, "I suppose we could draw the shutters, instead, but it would make the room feel close and old-fashioned."

"I understand completely." Caspar glanced down at the paper, and then up at a shelf where he had some cloth he thought might serve. Narrowing his eyes briefly, he gauged the available fabric against what he could see would be needed, and said with a smile, "I believe I can have those for you before the start of next week, if that is soon enough." He quickly jotted a figure on the paper and handed it back. "I believe that the cost will also be satisfactory."

She glanced at the paper and nodded briskly. "It will have to be. That will give me time to scrub the walls and try to get the smell of smoke out of the room." Sighing, she added fiercely, "I hope to encounter that fellow again some day. I will give him such a shake that he will be lucky to leave with his teeth still in his head."

She sniffed and waved a hand dismissively. "That is not your concern, I know."

"On the contrary, madame, I am grieved for your trouble, but also glad for your good fortune that the damage was not greater."

Anke frowned. "You have a way, Mister Schmidt, of always finding some good in things, no matter how challenging they may be." Her face broke into a wide smile as she added, "I am glad for that, as it likely saved my husband's life."

Caspar said nothing, but bowed in acknowledgment.

Anke squared her shoulders and stepped toward the door. Pausing at the verge, she looked outside and said, "Why, you are right. It is a glorious day. It feels as though the world is finally ready to start anew, unburthened by the errors of the past. Long may it remain that way."

Caspar bowed again, and called to her as she departed, "A worthy hope indeed. Good day to you, madam."

Also in Audiobook

Many readers love the experience of turning the pages in a paper book such as the one you hold in your hands. Others enjoy hearing a skilled narrator tell them a story, bringing the words on the page to life.

Brief Candle Press has arranged to have *The Bridge* produced as a high-quality audiobook, and you can listen to a sample and learn where to purchase it in that form by scanning the QR code below with your phone, tablet, or other device, or going to the Web address shown.

Happy listening!

tfar.us/TheBridgeAudio

Historical Notes

The months just after American independence was finally formalized were surprisingly bleak for most citizens of the new nation. The runaway hyperinflation of the fiat Continental currency has made an appearance as a plot device in several of my books—most particularly *The Will*, where my main character made a sly use of it for some sharp dealing—but the broader impacts on the economy were widely negative.

I wanted to explore some of the other challenges that attended independence, not the least of which was the question of reconciliation between people who had been on the opposite sides of the war. The natural confrontation between a former prisoner of war and a deserter made for a powerful place to begin that exploration, but I wanted to also acknowledge that there were people who had leaned toward the Crown without taking up arms, too.

Add in the historical tension between the Swedish settlers of *Nya Sverige* (New Sweden) and the Dutch settlers who largely displaced them in Delaware, plus the complexities of shifting religious practices and affiliations, and there was an awful lot of conflict for a place where peace had just broken out.

While *Nya Sverige* was a generation and more removed from the rise of the American Revolution, I know from my own family that many people cling to the old ways when that is all that remains to remind them of their origins as they make their way in a strange land.

It may seem as though I indulged in some unnecessary roughness against poor Caspar when he contracted lockjaw, but it was one of the hazards that we tend to overlook in the modern day. It would have completely upended—if not outright ended—someone's life at the time, and the chance misfortune also set up the opportunity to illustrate the community rallying to Caspar's support.

Studying the modern clinical presentation of lockjaw—more commonly known today as tetanus—was sobering stuff, and trying to describe how it would have been to experience as an 18th century patient was literally the stuff of nightmares.

The symptoms of rigid, spasming muscles are caused by a neurotoxin that is released by the ubiquitous bacterium *Clostridium tetani.* The infection itself thrives in the absence of oxygen, and so the lancing of Caspar's toe based on the then-current medical theory of the humours was coincidentally a beneficial treatment.

Modern medicine adds to this with antitoxins and powerful antibiotics to kill the bacterium off, but absent those interventions, the course of the disease is, as closely as I could learn, similar to what I depicted Caspar enduring. Most notably, although the toxin produced by the bacterium interferes with the operation of nerves, it apparently has no direct effect on the function of the brain, which means that sufferers typically go through the experience conscious and aware of their torment.

Fortunately, most readers will already be current on their tetanus shots—and if not, let this story serve as motivation to make an appointment today. Untreated, tetanus kills about a quarter of its victims. With modern medical support, that number only comes down to about fifteen percent. Terrible odds for a wholly preventable disease.

The hazards that attend open windows and children are, sadly, timeless, and while I did not relish killing off Betje, her loss drove the final reconciliation between two men who otherwise might have spent the rest of their lives making each other miserable. It also allowed me to show how all reconciliation starts with acknowledging the humanity of our opponents. It is a lesson that is, itself, timeless.

Acknowledgements

For the past seventeen years, I have had a Halloween ritual of sitting down and starting to write on the stroke of midnight, accompanied by thousands of other writers around the world. National Novel Writing Month was a community, a set of accountability partners, and, most importantly, a framework that ensured that I would plow through no less than 1,667 words every day. It was ingrained in my writing process and habits, and there are several books in this series that might never have reached your hands without NaNoWriMo.

This year, after suffering a series of scandals that should have been avoidable, NaNoWriMo announced that they will cease to exist. I do not anticipate that the loss of this organization will substantially change my process, but I wanted to gratefully acknowledge the role that this crazy idea had in helping me to become the novelist I am today. Thanks for the online get-togethers, the in-person celebrations, and the wonderfully off-kilter kickoff meetings, WriMos.

I'll miss them when midnight rolls around this Halloween.

Thank You

I deeply appreciate you spending the past couple of hundred pages with the characters and events of a world long past, yet hopefully relevant today.

If you enjoyed this book, I'd also be grateful for a kind review on your favorite bookseller's Web site or social media outlet. Word of mouth is the best way to make me successful, so that I can bring you even more high-quality stories of bygone times.

To hear about my newest releases, appearances, special offers, and more, sign up for my monthly newsletter at https://tfar.us/newsletter.

I'd love to hear directly from you, too — feel free to reach out to me via my Facebook page, Twitter feed, or Web site and let me know what you liked, and what you would like me to work on more.

Again, thank you for reading, for telling your friends about this book, for giving it as a gift or dropping off a copy in your favorite classroom or library. With your support and encouragement, we'll find even more times and places to explore together.

larsdhhedbor.com
Facebook: Lars.D.H.Hedbor
LarsDHHedbor on YouTube